JULIAN'S CAT

*The Imaginary History of
a Cat of Destiny*

JULIAN'S CAT

The Imaginary History of a Cat of Destiny

story and pictures

by

Mary E. Little

MOREHOUSE PUBLISHING
WILTON, CONNECTICUT

Morehouse Publishing Co.
78 Danbury Road
Wilton, Connecticut 06897

LIBRARY OF CONGRESS CATALOGING-IN-PUBLICATION DATA

Little, Mary E.
    Julian's cat: the imaginary history of a cat of destiny/told and illustrated by Mary E. Little.
        p. cm.
    Bibliography: p.

    ISBN 0-8192-1430-2

    1. Julian, of Norwich, b. 1342—Fiction. 2. Cats—Fiction. 3. Norwich (England)—History—Fiction. 4. Great Britain—History—14th century—Fiction.   I. Title.
PS3562.I78293J8   1989
813'.54—dc19   88-31750
                                                                        CIP

Printed in the United States of America
by
BSC LITHO
Harrisburg, PA

CONTENTS

AUTHOR'S ACKNOWLEDGEMENTS

My deepest gratitude is extended to those people who have given immeasurable help to me in the preparation of this story: Robert Llewelyn, Chaplain of the Julian Shrine in Norwich and author of books and articles about Julian of Norwich, who provided me with priceless books and materials—and encouragement; the Reverend Mother Violet, C.A.H. Ditchingham, who gave me richly of her knowledge of Fourteenth Century Norwich and her own writings; the Reverend Father John-Julian, O.J.N. USA; Canon Michael McLean, and Anthony Beck of the Dean and Chapter's Library, Norwich Cathedral; and the staffs of the Norfolk County Library, Norwich Division, Local Studies Department; the University of Arizona Main Library; and the Tucson Public Library U.S.A.

From the innumerable titles of works consulted in the writing of this book, I list only a selection:

Primary source of Mother Julian's words of counsel: *Julian of Norwich: Showings*, translated from the critical text with an introduction by Edmund College, O.S.A. and James Walsh, S.J., Paulist Press, New York, 1978.

Jewson, Charles B., *People of Medieval Norwich*, Jarrold and Sons, Ltd., Norwich, 1956.

Pelphrey, Brant, *Love Was His Meaning: The Theology and Mysticism of Julian of Norwich*, Salzburg Studies in English Literature, Salzburg, Austria, 1982.

Rickert, Edith, *Chaucer's World*, Columbia University Press, New York, 1948.

Sansbury, Ethelreda, *An Historical Guide to Norwich Cathedral*, Dean and Chapter of Norwich, 1981.

Saunders, H.W., *An Introduction to the Obedientiary and Manor Rolls of Norwich Cathedral Priory*, Jarrold and Sons, Ltd., Norwich, 1930.

Sayer, Frank Dale, ed., *Julian and her Norwich: Commemorative Essays and Handbook to the Exhibition "Revelations of Divine Love,"* Julian of Norwich 1973 Celebration Committee, Norwich, 1973.

Wilkins, Nigel, *Music in the Age of Chaucer*, D.S. Brewer, Cambridge, England, 1970.

FOREWORD

In St. Savior's Chapel in Norwich Cathedral there is a stained glass window which honors one of the greatest of all mystics, Julian of Norwich. She holds in her hands her book *Revelations of Divine Love*. And at her feet, staring boldly out at the human race, sits, possessively, a cat.

Little is known about Julian of Norwich; nothing at all about Julian's cat.

He *must* have a story.

With love and humility I offer this one.

Mary E. Little
Spring 1989

DEDICATION

To Buster,
the handicapped stray
who brought joy
to my anchorhold.

PART I

N THE
MERCHANT'S
HOUSE

e was born in a litter of five on a woolpack.

A merchant kept the mother cat there in his cellar storeroom to rid the place of mice and vermin.

Nick, the merchant's youngest apprentice, heard him say that the kittens were to be put into a meal sack and dropped into the Wensum River so that the mother cat could continue her work, free from the demands of offspring. And Nick was afraid that he would be the one ordered to do the deed.

The two older apprentices had important work to do, so the small, often unpleasant tasks and all the fetching and carrying were left to Nick. When William, the eldest apprentice, provided him with a meal sack and told him to look sharp about it and be back at the storeroom before dark, Nick knew it would be useless to object.

The Mother cat did not object when Nick knelt beside the woolpack and stroked her as he watched the kittens nurse. His was a familiar hand. Whenever he was helping to load or stack or unload or move merchandise in the storeroom, he would steal a moment to stroke her and talk to her. She was a tawny yellow tabby with golden eyes, and on her forehead was the mark of feline nobility, the tabby mark of "M."

The kittens were not much bigger than mice. Three were gray, one was black, and one was tawny yellow. Their eyes were shut tight but their mouths and tiny paws continued to move as he picked them up one by one and laid them in the bottom of the sack.

Outside the dark, stuffy storeroom the air was crisp with the first hint of autumn, and the leaves on the trees were beginning to change color. King Street was teeming with merchants, monks and friars, wagoneers and carters, housewives and servants, pilgrims and other travelers, and it was noisy with cries of mountebanks, sellers of fake medicines, and peddlers.

"Fresh fish! Just caught at dawn!"

"Tasty ribs o' beef. Come buy, come buy!"

"A ribbon for your sweetheart! And laces for her gown! Come buy!"

"Here, you, lad. I've a treasure o' relics straight from the Holy Land. A sliver o' wood from the True Cross! Three threads from the Virgin's mantle! Or for two pence, a drop o' bloody sweat—"

Nick elbowed his way past the man with palms stitched on his hat, crossed into Tombland, the ancient market place, and slipped through St. Ethelbert's Gate into the Cathedral Close. He paused by the Chapel of St. Mary-in-the-Marsh, and lingered to admire the ivy-covered stone of its ancient walls, then slowly walked over to the canal. Bargemen were busy with slabs of stone being delivered to the Benedictine monks at the cathedral. Repairs to the cloisters, burnt out over a century before, had been halted by the ravages of the plague that men called the Black Death. But now the monks had started rebuilding again. Nick watched the men as they worked in their short, ragged, sweat-soaked kilts, or with bare torso and legs so as not to risk damage to a jerkin.

Nick dawdled on his way along the canal to the watergate and stood on the riverbank. The Wensum was crowded with boats and barges—wool coming down the river, corn going up the river. He sat down on a grassy knoll, putting off as long as possible the drowning of those kittens.

Why should he care? Why should he care so much about what happened to those little scraps of felinity?

The older apprentices had chided him about his concern for the mother cat.

"You best leave that animal be. Some folk hereabout believe cats be o' the devil. Satan's creatures. Only witches and sorcerers put them on cushions and feed them men's food."

"Aye, cats be only for keeping down mice and vermin. Else they be gathered up and sold to Wat the Furrier."

Nick thought of the cat that had shared his bed and bowl and trencher, his bread and meat, and his short hours of playtime when he was a small child in the nearby village of Conesford. Cats were for love and loving. He'd make a song of that—someday.

Nick owed much to the merchant, but he was not happy as his apprentice. He knew that he could never be happy in the merchant's trade. In fact, he loathed it. He loathed the very thought of spending his life dealing with *things*, and the cost of *things*, and the price of *things*, and the buying and selling of *things*, when all he wanted to do was make songs and sing them. He longed to be in the new Song School at Norwich Cathedral, but now he had no hope for that. His whole family in Conesford had been taken by the plague while he was memorizing his *Donatus* in the grammar school. That was when the merchant, a friend of his father's, had taken him in as apprentice.

And that was when he went to see the Lady Julian. Mother Julian. He desperately needed a mother's guidance and had no one else to turn to.

Not that anybody could "see" the Lady Julian. She lived in an anchorhold, small lodgings or cell attached to St. Julian's Church in Conesford, where she had vowed to stay for the rest of her life. Some folk believed that she took the name of Julian from the church when she came to make her home there. No one could see her, but one might speak with her through her window, a window covered by a black curtain with a white cross in the middle. She would come to her window and speak from behind her curtain, and one could hear her and receive her comfort and guidance, for she was known to be very holy. She never turned anyone away, not even a boy of fourteen summers.

Nick told Mother Julian of his distaste for the merchant's trade, and of his love for music and his longing to be in the Song School at the cathedral. She bade him have patience with his lot for the time being, and not to run away as he wanted to, for in the end, she said, all would be well.

"Pity and love protect us in our time of need," she told him, and advised him to wait and see what pity and love, received and given by him, could do.

So Nick tried to be patient and to content himself by strumming the strings of his gittern and singing softly in the evenings as he sat on his straw-filled pallet, where the apprentices slept at the back of the showroom.

Now as he sat on the grassy knoll, he wondered if pity and love for a kitten might be of any value at all.

He closed his eyes and longed to stretch out on the grass for he was tired, and the sun had just broken out from behind the smoky gray clouds. The wind that ruffled his hair was laden with smells, sometimes a whiff of cesspool and midden, compost and refuse, often the heavy smell of malt from the cathedral brewery.

Malt! The *granary!*

Nick was almost startled by his own sudden idea. He jumped to his feet and ran back the way he had come until he reached St. Mary-in-the-Marsh, then turned right and ran to the row of small buildings at the back of the cathedral cloisters, the buildings that housed the stables, the bakery, the brewery—and the granary.

An old monk, Brother Giles, was sitting in the doorway of the granary, nodding in the warming sun.

Breathless, Nick dropped to his knees beside him and laid the sack in his lap.

"God's greeting, Brother," Nick panted. "Oh, please, Brother, please, have you here a mother cat? A nursing cat? One that might be willing to suckle orphans?" He pulled open the sack so the monk could see the contents.

Brother Giles chuckled and rubbed his pate. "Here? In the *granary?* Come see."

He heaved to his feet and, followed by Nick, stepped inside the granary. As they moved, kittens of all sizes and colors scattered before them like a spray of water when a stone is cast into a pool.

"You'd best stay in the doorway, lad," the monk said. "These are wild ones. Let us see—"

Nick watched from the doorway as the old monk

made his way toward the back, where a big grey cat lay on a sack full of malt, sleepily staring at them through half-closed eyes. The monk slowly removed the kittens from the sack he carried and laid them carefully in front of the cat.

She roused.

She sniffed them over.

Slowly the monk retreated, walking away backward toward Nick.

The cat began to lick the kittens. She licked them all, each one all over. Then, after shoving them about with her forehead and nose, she rolled over on her side. Nick and Brother Giles left quietly as the kittens began to nurse.

The sun was low when Nick returned to the store-room. He reported to William, who set him immediately to another task. Nick opened a pack of baldricks from Italy, handsome leather belts, some worked with silver ornaments, others with semi-precious stones. He carefully laid them out side by side on a large tray to be taken upstairs to the merchant, who would look them over and select some of the finest to display in his shop. But before it became quite dark Nick slipped around to the place where the mother cat lay. There was just enough light from the doorway for him to see her clearly, stretched out on the woolpack.

Nick grinned.

Not easily discernible to the casual observer, but

plain enough to one who knew what he was looking for, lay the tawny yellow kitten, pressed against the belly of his tawny yellow mother, sucking lustily.

* * * * *

He was eight weeks old when his mother finished weaning him, and Nick was hard put to keep him fed and out of mischief. Of course the other apprentices had discovered him, and they warned Nick repeatedly to get rid of him, for the master would be very angry if he discovered that Nick had disobeyed him and failed to carry out his orders completely.

He was ten weeks old when the merchant discovered him.

* * * * *

The storeroom was actually the cellar of the merchant's home. The ground floor served as his office and showroom where his merchandise could be displayed: bolts of fine cloth, leather baldricks of expert workmanship, collars made of gold chain, and brooches made of silver and gold, some set with precious stones. The merchant usually sent William, who assisted him in the shop, to the cellar when new supplies were brought in or when he wanted some special item brought up to the showroom. He went himself only on occasion to check conditions there. The day he came down and discovered Nick fondling the tawny yellow kitten would have been one of disaster for the youth had the merchant not been followed down by his little daughter, Cecily.

The merchant had grabbed the kitten by the scruff of its neck with one hand and had raised the other hand for a blow to Nick's ear when Cecily squealed and ran in front of him.

"Oh! How sweet! How dear it is. Please, I would stroke it."

She stood on tiptoe and gently touched the kitten.

"Cecily! Why are you come down here? Have I not forbidden you to enter this place?"

The merchant's attention shifted from Nick to the little girl. He held his hand while Nick held his breath and Cecily held up both hands toward the kitten.

"I would hold it. Here, please, Father, let me have it."

And Nick slowly let out his breath as the merchant placed the yellow kitten in the child's hands. Ten-week-old kittens have ever been exquisite, lovely, and charming. The tawny yellow kitten with its downy fur, velvety ears, and dark-rimmed golden eyes was immediately adorable. Cecily held it up before her face, then cuddled it against her neck. The kitten reached out a paw and gently batted at a lock of her hair.

"Cecily! Child, answer me. Why are you down here in the cellar?"

"Oh, Father, is it not sweet? Oh, Father, may I keep

it? Please? Please give Nick a penny so that I might have it for my own. Please! *Please!*"

"Answer me, Cecily, this instant! Why have you come down here when I have forbidden you—"

"Oh—well—I—I just wanted to see you Father, I was lonely, and I wanted to hear you say I am your darling, your sweet one, and—and you came down here—and—I just followed you."

Cecily held the kitten up before him.

"See how beautiful it is! I want it for my own. Please, Father. Pay Nick and I will take it upstairs and give it milk and it may sit on my chair and sleep on my bed and—please, please!"

"*Pay* Nick! Aye, he should be paid with a dozen lashes for disobedience."

Nick dropped to one knee, folded his hands, and raised his eyes to his master.

"Forgive me, Sire." he begged. "Pray, pardon me. See, he—the kitten—is the same color as his mother and, Sire, I, I . . ."

Nick could make an excuse for himself, but he could not lie. He hoped the merchant would somehow think that he had just overlooked the kitten, not singled him out to be saved.

"You see, Sire, when he was nursing, one could barely tell—"

"Enough, enough!" The merchant looked at his little daughter as she cuddled the kitten. If it would bring her joy, she should have the kitten. Her thin, pale little face was alight with pleasure. There was almost a tinge of pink in her cheeks.

"My child shall have the kitten. As for you—" he pulled Nick to his feet. "For the sake of your father who was the friend of my youth, I will spare you the lash. See that you obey in full, henceforth, or—"

"But, Father," Cecily interrupted. She looked up at him, her great, dark eyes stretched wide. "Nick was loving the kitten. He will miss him, I am sure. Please, may we give Nick something?" The lonely little girl had seen Nick daily as he sat with the apprentices at mealtime, but had never spoken with him. Now the two had something in common. Perhaps they could share talk about the kitten, share delight in the kitten's capers, share in the kitten's play. "And please, Father," she went on. "May Nick fetch me from school sometimes? And play ball with me in the garden? Please, Father. May he—"

"Now, now, Cecily. Enough for one time. Take your kitten upstairs and make your peace with Nurse about him. And I will settle with Nick."

Cecily kissed her father's hand and waved to Nick and then ran upstairs with the kitten.

* * * * *

The kitten revelled, not only in total freedom to indulge his curiousity and explore and discover all kinds of interesting nooks and corners in the merchant's house, but also in the cuddling and feeding and pampering by all the persons in the household.

"Ah! How beautiful he be!" cried one housemaid. "Look at that little tail. Strait up means happy. A sweet, friendly, happy little cat."

"And that mark on his forehead," said another. "Folk say that means something special. Look you—he butted my ankle with that mark, mind you! He likes me. Oh, the dearie little beast, he likes me!"

Everyone, that is, except for Cook, who found him a terrible nuisance, and Nurse, who did not like cats.

"Cats be evil!" Nurse wailed. "They be witches' creatures and fit only to keep cellars free of mice."

"Cats be lovely!" Cecily answered back, pert and saucy as she was because she was the merchant's only child and had no mother to guide her. "He shall be my companion, my playmate, my lively toy. And that shall be his name. Toy!"

But Nurse refused to be won over.

he merchant's house was larger than most of the houses in Norwich, because the merchant was a rich man. There were tiles on the roof and tapestries on the walls and fresh rushes on the floor. Two carved high-backed chairs stood among many settles and benches and stools in the large hall, which was the main room of the house. One chair was very high-backed and very richly carved and held a velvet cushion. The other was not so high-backed and not so richly carved, but it too held a velvet cushion and it belonged to Cecily.

Against one wall was a large cupboard or buffet that held many valuable vessels of pewter and silver. Opposite the cupboard was a great stone fireplace with a wide hood, one of the first in Norwich that had a chimney to carry smoke up above the roof. And a heavy carved table held three books, richly bound, with silver clasps. One was a psalter with beautiful colored pictures in the margins and initial letters of gold. The merchant was determined to enjoy all the luxuries of good living that had once been enjoyed only by the nobility. He could afford them.

At dinnertime, two trestle tables were set at the far end of the hall, one on a low platform with the two high-backed chairs for the merchant and his child, with Nurse on a stool by her side; the other table was set below on the floor for the apprentices and housemaids and other servants who were not serving the food. Sometimes guests might join them at the high table: a traveler, another merchant, a master craftsman, a minstrel, or even a pilgrim who had come by Norwich to consult the holy anchoress, Dame Julian, before continuing on his way to the great Shrine of the Most Holy Virgin Mary at Walsingham. And sometimes a craftman's apprentice or a laborer or some poor soul seeking alms would be served with the apprentices, for the merchant was a generous man.

The first dinnertime for Toy—and thereafter—he was allowed to frolic on the dinner table and taste of all that appealed to him, while the merchant watched, with indulgent amusement, his little daughter's delight and while Nurse glowered in disapproval and held her trencher well out of the kitten's reach.

"See how he eats, so dainty, from my hand!" Cecily

tilted her head toward Nurse. "He likes my frumenty and he likes my milk. And he likes to take bits of meat from my fingers. See?"

"Aye! I see all too well. And he will never have taste for mice, nor any hunger to catch them whilst he can eat his fill from your hand," Nurse grumbled. "Come now. Leave that nasty animal be, and let me wash your hands." She reached for a silver ewer shaped like a pelican with its beak open for the water to pour out, but Cecily pushed her hand aside.

"Not yet, Nurse, not yet. He has not finished his dinner." She pushed her trencher closer to Toy, who was lapping milk from a carved mazer, a wooden bowl. He ate the bits of meat and licked up the gravy, then sat back on his haunches by the saltcellar and began to wash.

When Toy finished washing, he tumbled his bulging little body to the rushes on the floor, sniffed and scratched and scrabbled among them and then relieved himself. He scratched again, covering his droppings, then romped among the rushes, leaping to catch a bit of dried blade he had stirred into the air. He frisked and frolicked his way across the hall until he came to the place where the old hound, Bruno, lay sleeping by the fireplace. He stood on his hind legs and pawed around Bruno's face. He licked Bruno's nose, then suddenly he dropped, sound asleep, between the old dog's big front feet. Bruno pulled himself up on all fours and stared down at the sleeping kitten. He looked up questioningly to his master, then back to the kitten, his old eyes stretched wide in astonishment. He lightly pawed the kitten, who mewed but did not wake. Then he lay down again and put his great muzzle by the kitten's tiny head.

From his place at the apprentices' table, Nick watched and smiled. The tawny yellow kitten was safe now.

"Oh, I do love him, I do," said Cecily. The child's eyes were fixed on Toy. He was entirely enchanting and lovable, inviting caresses and a share in his play. Her father's eyes grew sad as he thought of Cecily's mother, the sixteen-year-old bride he had brought home from Italy. Nurse's eyes, too, grew soft as she watched Cecily.

The child turned seven on Michaelmas, September 29. She was so frail, so small and delicate, Nurse wondered each day, as she walked with Cecily the long way to her ABC school at Carrow Priory, if all this education the master insisted on might be too much for her—she being only a little bit of a girl at that. Her father wanted her to have everything a child of nobility might have, but he would not permit her to live away from home. So she was sent each day to the nuns at Carrow to be given a fine lady's education. It was a long way to walk, there and back again, and most of the time Nurse had to carry her part of the way home.

Nurse could not make the merchant see that all this was too much for the child. He thought her perfect and would not admit that she seemed to be fading away before their very eyes, as her mother had, three years ago with the wasting Mediterranean sickness.

* * * * *

Children, particularly little girls, were not among Nick's favorite concerns. He was beginning to eye young maidens, with their rosebud mouths and newly curving outlines, with interest and pleasurable curiosity. In the past, when he had noticed Cecily at all from his place at the apprentices' table, he had thought the child was a boring, over-indulged little lass, and at first he expected her to be careless and perhaps a little rough with the kitten. He discovered to his surprise that the child, who could be a little tyrant on occasion, was gentle and loving with the kitten.

Nick soon found himself less and less in demand in the merchant's storeroom and more and more in attendance to the merchant's sad-eyed daughter. Anything was better than the dreary storeroom. He found it less than a chore to wait on the child, fetch her home from Carrow Priory, and share her games and playtime with Toy. He would always feel a sense of ownership in the tawny yellow kitten.

* * * * *

Toy grew rapidly. His beauty and grace were enhanced by the love and pampering lavished on him. His antics provided continual entertainment. When Christmastide festivities were at their height he was a center of attention among the merchant's guests.

Nick helped the child fasten a scarlet ribbon around his neck after dinner one day.

"Fetch the hourglass!" cried a draper seated next to the merchant at the high table. "I'll wager a penny he has that ribbon in shreds before a quarter of an hour be passed."

"Why, less than that. A groat if he do not tear it to pieces in half that time." The merchant laughed and tossed his coin onto the table.

Cecily pouted and blinked her big dark eyes, but Nick laughed when the merchant won.

The kitten grew accustomed to being handled by many different people. Even the entertainers who came in during the twelve days of feasting were amused and delighted with his friendliness and endless capering, and they all paid him much attention.

A small group of mummers came one day to act out the tale of Abraham and Isaac. The fellow who usually played the part of the Sacrificial Ram had stayed too long in his cups and was snoring under the servant's table when the play was ready to begin. Nick told Cecily to offer Toy for the part instead. They tried to tie a sprig of holly on the kitten's head for horns afterwhich Nick planned to hold a piece of evergreen in front of him for the thicket.

Before Nick could make the holly secure, Toy

demolished both horns and thicket and pulled off Abraham's beard. Roars of laughter from audience and actors alike did not bother him at all. He loved being the center of their attention.

Another day a minstrel came with his harp and sang songs and told stories. Nick sat at his feet, forgetful of Toy and the child and all else. And when the man paused to rest and drink a cup of ale, Nick told him how he himself longed just to make songs and sing them, songs about the people and things he knew and loved.

"There will come a need for your songs, lad, a growing hunger for them among ordinary folk," the ministrel said. "We are living in an age of tumult and disaster, and of change so rapid that folk can scarcely keep pace. Life is changing, our land is changing, even our language. English now is put down in writing! Why, I even heard a poet at the royal court reading his tales to the king and the nobles and their ladies—tales about ordinary folk, not kings and warriors, but a squire and a miller and a nun with her little dogs."

The man took a long swallow of ale and wiped his mouth with his sleeve. Then he smiled in remembrance as he spoke again.

"King Richard was much pleased—God rest his soul. Poor King Richard. Now there was a man who could appreciate a poem or a song. He did love poetry and tales and music. He wasn't much given to fighting wars." The minstrel shook his head sadly. "Now 'tis the other way 'round. This new king has no time or heart for happy, beautiful things."

The festivities continued through Twelfth Night.

A troupe of tumblers and acrobats performed somersaults and handsprings and dancing on stilts in the middle of the hall one evening.

It was the tumbling girl, who could stand balancing by her hands on the points of two swords held steady by her companions, who picked Toy from under the feet of the acrobats and carried him to Cecily.

"See, M'Lady," she said bowing, and she pointed to the "M" on his forehead. "A cat that bears that mark on his forehead, he be favored above others of his kind. That be a mark of honor. He be a great cat, a noble cat, an animal to be remembered and honored by all, if so be he live long enough!"

And seeing Cecily's delight at her words, the merchant tossed the tumbling girl a penny.

"A great cat, she said. A *noble* cat. Mark you, Nurse, he is one to be remembered. And honored."

Nurse only sniffed and turned her face away. She refused to stroke him, even when Cecily begged her.

"He belongs in the cellar, with dark evil creatures!" Nurse complained. "The very sight of him, the look and smell of him, frights me. Keep him from me, I pray you!"

But Toy was on friendly terms with the rest of the servants, even Cook, finally. When he got into mischief in the kitchen, playing among the ladies, hiding in an empty kettle, snatching a bit of sausage or a scrap of cheese, Cook swore at him and chased him and flapped at him with a cloth, but in the end usually saved him a tidbit from the platter and sometimes gave him a friendly scratch under the chin.

Only Nurse remained hostile, and that, of course, was a challenge to him to get the better of her as often as he could. He hid under the merchant's carved chair and when she walked past he jumped out at her and grabbed her ankle. Sometimes he suddenly jumped onto her lap, or onto her shoulder from behind, and the louder she screamed, the more he nuzzled her. And he afforded great sport to the entire household after dinner one day when he climbed up the back of her kirtle, her best gown, and hung on while she twisted and turned and screamed and cried but could not free herself of him. Cecily rescued Nurse and took him off and gave him a gentle scolding, but it did no good at all. He just tormented Nurse whenever he felt like mischief.

"He's a fiend, that cat!" she cried. "A creature of the devil, come straight from hell! May Our Lady and all the saints have mercy on us!"

he long, dark winter seemed less long, less dark to Nick and to Cecily because Toy was there, fast becoming a handsome, sturdy cat.

There were many days when the child could not go to school at all, sometimes because she had not the energy, sometimes because the streets were too foul with mud, the Norfolk winds too sharp, the drizzling rain and slushy snow too miserably cold.

The long Lenten fast was one long feast for Toy, for besides all the bits of raw fish given him by Cook, he got more and more from Cecily's trencher, as the child ate less and less. Nurse tried to make the master see that Cecily should be absolved from her fast, but he replied that she was not obliged to fast, and that she knew she could have anything she wanted at any time, and if she did not wish to eat, Nurse must not pester her about it.   * * * * *

One clear, mild day before Easter, Nick went to Carrow Priory to fetch Cecily home, and as they came down into King Street the child asked Nick about the tower on the hill to the northwest of them, the flint tower with a banner at the top rippling in the wind.

"That tower?" answered Nick. "Oh, that is the tower by the church where Mother Julian lives. And the banner is for sailors to see above the fog and over all the thick treetops and mark their course as they move along the Wensum. The tower shows pilgrims and other folk who need help the way to Mother Julian."

"And who may she be, this Mother Julian?" Cecily asked.

Nick told her about Dame Julian, Mother Julian. How she lived in her anchorhold, praying much of the time, giving counsel to those who sought her holy wisdom. "She talks much to God," Nick told her. "And it is said that sometimes God talks to her."

Nick took the child by the hand and turned north towards Tombland and the merchant's house, but she pulled back and look steadily at the tower.

"Will she, the Lady Julian—Mother Julian—will she speak with a child?" Cecily asked.

"Well—I don't know, Cecily. It does seem unwise, and probably unkind, to disturb her at her devotions.

Unless the matter be of great importance." Nick had never told anyone of his visit to the anchorhold, nor had he spoken through the black curtain again; but on several occasions he had slipped away and left a handful of hazelnuts or an apple or some other small offering on the gate leading to her cell. The one time he had her loving counsel, she gave him the courage and faith to believe that surely one day all would be well. And he knew that her motherly guidance would be there for him should he ever need it again. Now as he looked down into the child's great eyes, her grave little face reminded him that she, too, had no mother. Whatever wealth could bring her, she had—but she had no mother. Someday he might take her to Mother Julian.

"I would speak with her. Nick, please take me to speak with her." She pulled on his hand.

"Now? But Cecily, we will be late getting home and Nurse will be angry."

"Now. Nick, please. It *is* important. I have a question to ask her." She stopped and then went on almost in a whisper. "A question I dare not ask Nurse, or my father."

"But Cecily—"

"Now! Now, I say!" The child jerked Nick's arm and stamped her foot. "Now!"

Nick stood silent, unmoving, looking down at her. She had never behaved like this with him before.

Then, "Please, Nick, *please,* now! I beg you, Nick."

The distance to the anchorhold was not great, but the hill to the Tower was steep, and the way to it was along the main thoroughfare, crowded with people and animals, carts and horses, oxen, hawkers, traders, friars, and messengers. Stray cats and dogs, ravens, rats, even pigs rooted and scrabbled along the kennel, the gutter which ran down the middle of the street and was supposed to carry away sewage but was filled with garbage and refuse. They had to walk close to the buildings and avoid the center of the street for even housewives and kitchen maids cast their slops from upper-story windows into the kennel.

When they reached the gate of the anchorhold, Nick pulled a bell and an elderly servant came from the back of the cell, asking their business. At first she seemed unwilling to open the gate for them.

"The Lady Julian has been at that window all this blessed day. Folk won't leave her at peace for her prayers. Run along now and play your games and don't bother the holy anchoress!"

But Cecily raised her solemn eyes, which began to brim with tears.

"Only a moment, please! One question I must ask Mother Julian—and I won't come again, ever. Please, let me come in."

"The child has no mother," Nick found himself pleading. "She truly needs a word from Mother Julian."

"Very well. But mind you don't tease or be saucy.

28

Come." She opened the gate for them, and they approached the window with the black curtain.

Nick picked up Cecily and held her up to the curtain.

"No, Nick, No!" Cecily objected. "I must speak alone with Mother Julian. I can stand on tip-toe on this bench under the window and speak and hear. And Nick, you must go over to that side of the garden and you must not listen. Please Nick, promise you will not listen."

"Very well, Cecily. I will not listen." And Nick retreated as far away as he could in the small garden, wondering what problem Cecily had to lay before Mother Julian.

He turned his back and tried not to listen. He was aware of the voices of the child and the woman, although he could not distinguish the words, and at one point he thought Cecily was crying. He turned to look and saw Cecily's head bowed, her forehead on the sill with her two arms stretched across it reaching under the curtain.

And as he looked, a hand brushed the curtain aside, arms reached out and drew the child up so that she sat on the sill, cradled against the woman's breast. Nick could not see Mother Julian's face, for her head was bent over the child's. He was reminded of a painting of the Holy Mother and Child he had seen in the church of St. Peter Parmentergate. It was only with great effort that he could tear his gaze away and turn his back again.

After a while the voices ceased. The curtain was still and Cecily turned and sat down on the bench. Tears were drying on her cheeks, but she smiled as Nick approached her.

"And did Mother Julian answer your questions?" he asked.

"Oh, yes," Cecily told him. "Oh, yes."

He remembered Lady Julian's words to him less than a year past: "Pity and love protect us in our time of need." Pity and love received and given.

"And—are you comforted?" he asked, wondering what had caused Cecily's distress.

"Oh, yes!" she answered. "I am not afraid anymore."

What had this child to be afraid of, cherished as she was by all in her father's house? Nick wondered but was somehow reluctant to intrude on the child's privacy by asking. Yet Nick also felt that he must ask if there might be any way he could help her.

"Cecily—" Nick tried. "Can you not tell me why or of what you have been afraid, or if there be some way I might help you?"

"No, Nick. There is no way you can help me. And I cannot tell you, for it would only make you sad, and I do not want you to be sad for me. But you will know, and I think you will understand some day—soon."

Nick felt sad for her now as he looked down into her big, sober eyes, her thin, pale face with its delicate pointed chin and tight little baby mouth.

As they walked down the hill Cecily stumbled twice. Nick picked her up and carried her all the way home.

oy did love the velvet cushion on Cecily's high-backed chair.

The chair usually stood by the big hooded fireplace in the hall and was moved to the dais only at dinnertime. When Toy was not playing with Cecily in her chamber or teasing Cook in the kitchen, he was often curled up in the chair, and the housemaids despaired of ever ridding the velvet cushion of tawny yellow hair, for Toy was old enough now to shed as the weather grew warmer. But the housemaids loved him, and were wont to play with him and share his capers so that it took both Nurse and Cook to keep them busy at their tasks. The household was a livelier, happier place because of Toy.

He followed Cecily wherever she went through the house and nudged her ankles with his forehead and rubbed himself against her legs. He loved the child. She was his person.

And he loved old Bruno. Occasionally his playfulness roused the old dog to respond. Bruno would roll over on his back and seem almost to juggle Toy on his great paws, and Toy would pull on the dog's ears and lick around his face until they both grew sleepy again.

On the few occasions when he was all by himself, and Bruno was drowsing by the fire, in no mood to play, he roamed around the hall looking for things to play with, for something to do. He spent some time on the wide sill of the window looking through the leaded panes down into the street, alive with people, carts, wagons, horses, dogs, pigs, and stray cats. When he tired of watching out the window, he amused himself by exploring again the objects on the shelves of the cupboard, where there were metal things, flagons and bowls of pewter and silver, and pottery vessels for him to knock around. When he broke a pottery cruet the housemaid was patient about cleaning up the mess, but the merchant was angry and threatened to get rid of him if he did it again. Sometimes he curled up in the lavatory, the basin in which folk who sat at the low table were supposed to wash their hands before eating their dinner.

But the velvet cushion in Cecily's chair was his very favorite thing.

At last one day the merchant acknowledged that his child was not as well as she should be. He gave her a gentle gray palfrey, a small pony-like creature, and Nick now walked beside her to and from Carrow Priory and steadied her in the cushioned seat on the animal's back. But when the nuns sent word to Cecily's father that she sorely needed a physician, he was all of a sudden beside himself.

"Why was I not warned of this before!" he demanded of Nurse, who had spent a whole year or more trying to make him see Cecily's decline. "My beautiful daughter! My only child!" He beat his fists together. "See you to it, Nurse, that she has every care to make her well. See that she lacks nothing." He paced the floor, tearing at his hair, then he stopped and grasped poor Nurse by the shoulders.

"By the Rood, don't let her out of your sight! Be watchful. Tend her carefully. Keep the coalfire alight in the brazier in her chamber. See that she be well covered at night!"

And he sent for the best leeches and physicians in Norwich, who rubbed the child with ointments and put poultices, hot plasters of pigeon's dung and honey, on her chest and made her swallow foul-tasting concoctions of musk and ambergris and dragon's blood. Sometimes she struck their hands away and shut her lips tight, refusing to take their remedies, but more often she was compliant, remarkably patient for a child so used to having her own way. It may be that she was often too weak to resist.

Now that she spent more and more time in her bed,

Toy lay in the crook of her arm, his head on her shoulder, one paw stretched to her neck. And in the few intervals when Nurse left them alone for a short time, Cecily talked to him as though he could understand what she said, and told him what she could not tell to Nurse or her father—or Nick.

"You must not be sad when I leave you," she said. "Cook and the maids will care for you and play with you and love you for my sake. I am not afraid anymore because Mother Julian explained to me how all will be well. How I will be filled with joy and bliss without end. And do you want to know what else she told me?" She scratched under his chin, and he stretched his neck and closed his eyes in his own kind of bliss. " 'As truly as God is our Father, so truly is God our Mother. Our Mother in nature.' That's what she said. 'Mother of life and of all things in nature.' Even you, Toy. Think of that! And she told me 'All shall be well, and I will see it for myself that every kind of thing shall be well. So I am not afraid anymore."

She stopped scratching his chin and took his head in her hands. "And you must promise, Toy, promise not to torment poor old Nurse so much. She really can't help it—here she comes!"

Nurse came in bearing a small pewter cup. "Now Cecily, drink this tansy posset. I've covered the bitter taste with honey. The tonic will do you good."

She set the cup down on a chest beside the bed and

plumped the pillows behind Cecily and pulled her up against them.

"Scat! Run off! Go away!" Nurse clapped her hands in Toy's face. He stared back at her and did not move.

"Evil creature! Now, Cecily, mind you drink it all. Don't leave any for that nasty cat." Nurse handed the cup to Cecily, then sat down on a stool by the bed.

Toy stared, unblinking, at Nurse and waited confidently until Cecily let him lick the last mouthful from her cup.

*　*　*　*　*

Spring came early that year. Sun began to pierce the smoky clouds by mid-morning, and the days became warmer, brighter, and longer.

The walled garden in back of the merchant's house was burgeoning into splashes of color against the fresh green of box and ivy and grass. Tulips from Holland and iris and early daisies were beginning to bloom, and the fruit trees espaliered against the wall of the building were full of buds; their branches, trained in graceful patterns, clung lovingly to the rough surface.

The beautiful sunny days which followed the rains of early spring were joy to Cecily. Nick, at her demand, was allowed to spend more time with her. When she asked to have her chair placed in the garden, so that she could play outdoors with Toy it was Nick (gittern hanging on his back, for she always asked for a song) who fetched it for her. And it was Nick who carried her down the stairs with Toy in her arms, followed by Nurse, who brought her blanket and her ball. She would sit in her chair in the garden and throw the ball for Toy, sheltered from the wind in an angle formed by the sleeping chambers above. The cat would not fetch it back to her. He batted it with his two front paws and chased it over the lawn and into the hedges, and Nick retrieved it and gave it back to her. When she tired of Toy's antics she held him in her lap and stroked him while Nurse told them a story.

Nurse and Nick sat on the ground in front of Cecily's chair. Nurse's stories were often of Queen Anne, who had caught her fancy and become her idol of all that was splendid and romantic and grand. For Nurse had stood among the crowds that memorable day when the young queen had visited the Great Hospital in Norwich.

"Never did I see the likes of her before, or hear tell of any like her," Nurse declared. "All dressed in velvet and satin and precious jewels, God rest her soul," and Nurse crossed herself, "and a great tall thing on her head with a thin, fine veil a-hanging from it and blowing in the breeze. All the fine ladies hereabouts had to have one like it afterwards, even though it must have been a chore to keep it on. And all the knights and ladies riding with her all a-glitter, too. But that was not the great wonder of her. Never can you guess the true marvel of her."

Here Nurse looked up at Cecily for a comment.

Nick threw Cecily a warning glance over Nurse's head.

"Never, Nurse," said Cecily, dutifully, although she and Nick had heard the story many times. "Tell us, please, Nurse, tell us of the marvel."

"Queen Anne, in all her finery, came riding *sideways* on her horse! Sideways, mind you, with her skirts flowing back along the pony's rump all graceful, like a banner." Nurse wiped her eyes.

"They do say King Richard wanted to destroy the palace where she died, poor young Queen. It is said he loved her very much. And well he might, so good and kind was she, tender young lady, too young to die." Here Nurse as usual burst into tears.

Cecily took advantage of Nurse's emotional pause. "Nick, please tune your gittern and sing us a song, one of your own songs, please."

Nick was very clever at composing songs, and besides singing the popular lays, he sometimes sang a song he had made himself.

"Make me a song, Nick," said Cecily. "Please sing me a song about—about cats. Sing me a song about a cat like Toy."

To Cecily's great astonishment—for she had meant to tease Nick and demand a song which would surely confound him—Nick began.

Fair dear cat of golden hue,
  Softly "purr," softly "mew."
Bringeth joy to me and you,
  Sing softly "purr."

Wonteth he to sit and dream,
  Softly "purr," softly "mew."
Liketh he a dish of cream,
  Sing softly "purr."

Sweet to touch, he gently plays,
  Softly "purr," softly "mew."
Humankind he ne'er obeys,
  Sing softly "purr."

He moveth folk to loving laughter,
  Softly "purr," softly "mew."
He giveth all his love thereafter,
  Sing softly "purr."

Clos-ed now his golden eyes,
  Softly "purr," softly "mew."
In your lap he quiet lies,
  Sing softly "purr,"
  Sing softly "purr,"
  "Purr,"
  "Purr,"
  "Purr."

"Oh, that was beautiful, Nick! Truly you are clever, and your singing is sweet to hear." Cecily lay back in her chair. "Sing it again. Please, Nick, I would hear it all over again. Do sing."

"Aye, sing—and keep singing—and keep making songs, Nick—Nicholas Tanner, is it?"

They were all three somewhat startled, for so engrossed had they been in Nick's song that they had not noticed the tall man who now stepped from the doorway onto the garden path and approached them.

Nick rose to his feet from where he had been sitting cross-legged on the grass and, speechless, nodded his head.

The man wore the habit of a Benedictine religious, and his thick blond hair surrounded a tonsured pate. He held out his hand toward Nick and introduced himself.

"I am Brother Wilfred, precentor of the cathedral priory. I have just come from a visit with Dame Julian, and I would like a word with you."

* * * * *

At first Nick thought he might not be able to leave the merchant's house and go to live with the monks in the Song School at the cathedral, not because the merchant was unwilling to release him, but because Cecily wailed and cried at the thought of his leaving.

Until the merchant told her that the precentor had learned of Nick through the anchoress, Lady Julian.

"I confess that I don't understand it," he said. "By the Rood, 'tis strange to me, how the recluse Dame Julian knew of Nick."

"Dame Julian? *Mother Julian?* Mother Julian wishes Nick to become a chorister?" Cecily stared up at her father. She was sitting in her chair by the fireplace, Toy on her lap, her big velvet cushion under her and a small one at her back and another one on a stool under her feet.

"Aye. So she told the precentor who is the authority in the Song School." He shook his head. "I wonder if it be because Nick's father's tannery was near the church by Dame Julian's anchorhold. So Dame Julian may have known some member of Nick's family. But how came she to know of Nick's whereabouts? Or to concern herself on his behalf?"

"Father, if Mother Julian says it is right for Nick, then—then Nick must go."

"So? You change your mind? You are willing to let Nick go because she—Mother Julian? *Mother Julian*, you say—! Cecily! How came you by knowledge of this anchoress, this Dame Julian?"

Cecily's lips were tight and she looked up at her father in anguish. She did not want to grieve him. She did not believe she could make him understand her fear, or the relief and comfort and counsel she had sought— and received—from Mother Julian.

"I learned of her," she whispered slowly, then spoke up more loudly. "I learned of her at school. The sisters at Carrow, they know all about Mother Julian." She was silent again for a moment, then "If Mother Julian says that Nick should go to the Song School, then—then I'm willing for him to go."

And her father could get her to say no more.

ick found life at the cathedral Song School much more demanding than at the merchant's house, but he loved it. He was happy in spite of the long hours of study, the chores and errands he was expected to do in the cathedral, and the plain, but plentiful food. He was more than pleased when Brother Wilfred arranged for him to study polyphonic music and composition, in addition to Latin, rhetoric, writing, and plainsong.

Among the chores assigned to him, at the old monk's request, were helping Brother Giles plant flowers here and there around the cathedral and helping him in the granary, so that the two of them could indulge in endless talk about cats. Instead of being sent to drown kittens, Nick was now sent with the kittens—when there were too many in the granary—to butchers and bakers and mercers and drapers and other townspeople who bought them, usually in pairs, to mouse their premises. He must be always watchful to keep them out of the hands of the furriers, and out of the cathedral.

There was not much time for leisure in the everyday routine of the Song School, but the many saints' days and other holydays provided frequent breaks in the school routine, and an outlet for the boys to explode into sports and games. Nick, with Kit, the goldsmith's son, and Robyn the oblate, who expected to become a Benedictine monk some day, made a threesome. They shared everything from wrestling on the green to teasing the girls in the market place.

One of the liveliest feast days came on the twenty-third of April, St. George's Day. A brilliant procession wound through the streets of Norwich, and the boys of the Song School marched with the precentor.

The city's most prominent citizens were in the procession: the Bishop of Norwich, members of the nobility, the gentry, knights and squires, as well as merchants, craftsmen, and traders. There were minstrels and jugglers and other attendants, too, but the main attraction was "The George," a man in armor on horseback, and most especially, the Dragon. The George rode in continual combat with the Dragon, who cavorted from side to side, shook his canvas head, switched his canvas tail, blew smoke from his red-painted nostrils, and roared mightily, because there was a man inside him to make him do all these things.

Nick and Robyn and Kit argued much about how best to spend the rest of their free day after the procession—chasing maidens or wrestling on the green. They finally agreed that they could do both, and the argument now became which they should do first. As they donned their red St. George's surplices, Kit shouted, "I say we wrestle—and the winner be free to go first after the prettiest lass!"

"Ha! They all look alike to Robyn," Nick cried. "So let us find the girls first, and save our punches. What say you, Robyn?"

"I say we'd best be quick to get to our places. Look! Here comes Brother Wilfred."

"Sing well today, lads," said the succentor, assistant to Brother Wilfred, as he began to line the ten boys up in pairs.

"Aye, sing! And Keep singing!" The precentor called out gaily as he joined them. "Sing and keep singing!"

Nick suddenly stood still.

Brother Wilfred stepped over to him. "What ails you, lad?" he asked peering into Nick's face. "Do you see a ghost? Come along."

Nick looked up at him.

"That is what you first said to me—in the merchant's garden that day. 'Sing and keep singing.'"

"Yes? Well?"

"The little one there, in the garden, I have not thought of her since I came here. She is not well."

"Ah, yes. The sad-eyed child."

"She told me, often, that she hoped—she longed to see this procession today. Her father is a standard-bearer in the procession. He always rides close to the window and bows to her." Nick bowed his head in sudden shame that he had not thought of Cecily during his new life at the cathedral. What had happened to the pity and love of which Mother Julian had spoken?

Brother Wilfred studied Nick. "And what is it that you would do now?" he asked.

"Go there, if I may, Brother Wilfred, go and find out how she fares."

The child was overjoyed to see Nick, so much so that Nurse had to give in to her demand to take her out of bed so that she might watch the procession from the big window in the hall and wave to her father as he came riding by.

Nick drew her chair close to the window that was now opened onto the street. Then he piled the window seat high with cushions so that she could kneel there and lean easily over the wide sill and see everything in the street. She held Toy in her arms, and when he tried to prance on the sill and peer over the edge, she pulled him back.

"Nurse, please find my long cord, my green latchet, and bring it here to me. Nick, help me fashion a lead to hold him by. I'm so fearful that he may fall and be hurt."

"Child, don't you know that if he falls he'll land on his feet? His kind always do," Nurse remarked, and then added "the little varmint."

"Aye, but I'm sure it would hurt him sorely!" Cecily replied. "Listen! Here they come. I hear the bagpipes and the flutes!" She held the latchet, one end tied around Toy's neck, the other wound around her wrist, then they all, Toy included, leaned over the window sill.

It was well that Toy was anchored to something, for amid the noise of pipes and tabors, shawms and bombards, cymbals and singing and cheering, it seemed that all the dogs of Norwich (except for Old Bruno snoring by the fireplace) ran alongside the marchers, in and out among their feet, dodging the horses' hooves, barking and yapping excitedly. When the sun broke through the clouds it shone on brilliant colors of livery and festive raiment and banners snapping in the breeze, and glinted off the gilt and silver and brass of ornaments and trumpets and horns. It was enough to make people shout and want to jump up and down and dance, and enough to drive a little cat wild.

The merchant, resplendent in red velvet with two roses worked in gold on the breast of his doublet, rode so close to the window that the child could almost reach out and touch the swinging golden tassels on the banner he carried.

After Cecily's father had bowed and waved to her, and the rest of the procession had passed by, and the George and the Dragon with his antics were out of sight, she slid back into her chair and closed her eyes.

"I would lie down now," she said. She reached out and took Nick's hand and pressed it to her cheek. "I am so glad you were with us today, Nick," she added.

Nick looked down into the child's great dark eyes. Their hunger seemed to devour all the rest of her thin little face. And Nick's heart twisted within him. Pity and love—pity and love. Was he able only to receive, never to give?

He knelt by her chair and put his arms around her and cradled her against his shoulder. She seemed smaller, thinner than ever before.

"I too am glad I was here," he told her. "I am glad Brother Wilfred let me come today. I will try to see you—try to be with you—"

"Come, Cecily," Nurse interrupted. "I will carry you back to your bed now."

"Goodbye, Nick. Goodbye, dear Nick." Cecily drooped down into her cushion.

Nurse waved aside Nick's offer to carry the child. He closed the window, took the latchet off Toy, and quietly left the house.

* * * * *

Toy was banished from Cecily's chamber.

46

He lay curled up on his beloved velvet cushion in Cecily's chair, but he was not asleep. From the vantage point of the chair he watched the constant coming and going of strange people.

No one had thought to feed him.

The high table was not set up because the master was being served in his own chamber. It was Cook who, at the end of the second day, brought a bowl of frumenty with some shreds of meat in it and set it on the floor by the chair. He ate only a little. He hadn't taken kindly to his eviction by the leeches, and he was too discomfited to be hungry.

The child had barely moved or opened her eyes since Nurse put her back to bed on St. George's Day.

One after the other the leeches came and went, each man swearing by his own special saint, by his own special potion, from Gracia Dei to shavings of gold in hot wine. On the third day after St. George's Day all the leeches and physicians came together. It was the visitation of this last group that afforded Toy re-entry into Cecily's chamber.

They all seemed to be arguing with one another, and Cecily's father was arguing with all of them, and when Toy saw the door left ajar in the confusion, he took advantage of the situation to slip back in. Having been so rudely removed from the bed so many times, he knew better than to jump up there while Nurse or anyone else could see him. So he slid behind a chest and bided his time.

He had a long wait.

After a priest and his acolyte had come and gone, Cecily's father stood a long, long time staring down at his child, then he knelt by the bed for a long time, then he pulled up a stool and sat for a long time. Nurse sat all the while on the trundle bed, which slid by day under Cecily's and was pulled out at night beside it. Nurse sat fully clothed, leaning her head against the coverlet, trying to stay awake, watching the child.

There were few sounds from the street outside because it was dark now and there were never any lights out there, except from Christmas Eve to Epiphany, and few folk ventured out after the eight o'clock curfew. It wasn't until the merchant heard faintly the cathedral bell ringing the hour of midnight that he rose, knelt again by the bed, then tip-toed out.

Toy approached from the side opposite to the lightly dozing Nurse, jumped onto the bed, burrowed under Cecily's elbow into the crook of her arm, and put his head on her shoulder, his paw against her neck. The child stirred and turned her head so that her cheek rested on the "M" on his forehead.

The quiet of pre-dawn was shattered by Nurse's shrieks, then came the cries and hubbub of the rest of the household and Bruno's long, mournful whimpering.

Nurse burst into the hall holding Toy aloft at arm's

length by the scruff of his neck—the first time that she had ever touched him.

"Fiend! Witch's varmint! He killed our Cecily—sucked the breath out of her! There she lies, dead because of him!"

She tore open the window and the shutter.

"Begone! Get you back to hell whence you came! Out, murderer! Out, you devil, out!"

And she flung him through the window out into the street.

PART II

STRAY IN
NORWICH

e landed on his feet and it hurt him sorely.

For a while he lay still in the kennel in the middle of the street. It was foul with refuse. When he finally tried to move it hurt him so that he howled. And he continued to howl for somebody to come help him. He did not know where he was or what had happened to him; he only knew that he hurt and needed help and that no one came to help him. He howled again and again.

In the dark house opposite the merchant's a shutter banged open.

"Stop yer howling! Be still and let honest folk sleep! Scat!" And a pailfull of water was thrown down on him.

He pulled himself up and tried to shake free of the water, but pain made the effort useless. In spite of it he dragged himself away from the kennel and huddled wet and shivering and hurting against the wall of the house. He had never been wet or cold or hurt before. He had never even been outdoors before, except for the walled garden behind the merchant's house. He mewed piteously but no one came. No Cecily. No Cook. No housemaid. No Nick.

He could see no cover. There was nothing to crawl under because the walls stood flush with the street. He crawled along the wall until he came to a door slightly recessed in the wall but closed. He could not walk on his left front foot for the pain was too great, and he ached all over. He tried to wash himself but finally gave up and just huddled whimpering in a corner of the doorway.

He heard footsteps and raised his head, hoping that help had come to him. A lantern swung over him.

"Cat!" muttered a grating, unfamiliar voice. "All that noise be a cat." The toe of the man's boot probed Toy's aching side and he cried out. "Hush your noise! When my watch be done with I'll fetch a meal sack from the baker. That dirty yellow hide might be worth somethin' from the furrier." The watchman swung his lantern away and plodded on down the street.

Soon after the cathedral bell rang the Angelus at daybreak, sleepy servants and water-carriers began to pass by with yoke-and-pails or leather bottles, going to the well. Carts began to rumble up and down the street. Men pushed wheelbarrows filled with produce for the market, and horse-drawn wagons clattered over the cobblestones. The noise increased with the shouts of wagoneers and carters, and to this clamor was added the raucous barking of a big dog.

The dog, thin and ragged-eared, came scrabbling down the kennel. He heard the cat crying and loped over to him, not with affection like old Bruno, but snarling and baring his teeth. The cat cowered into the corner and, as the dog snorted over him, Toy for the first time in his life hissed and instinctively struck out at the dog's muzzle with the extended claws of his right paw. The dog recoiled, shaking his head, then lumbered back to the kennel.

And now Toy felt something else that he had never felt before. It was worse than the cold, worse than the wet, worse than the pain.

It was fear.

* * * * *

He moved out of his corner and crawled slowly, painfully along the wall. It was a long time before he came to an open space between two buildings. He stayed close against the wall and followed it around the corner until he came to another door. This one was ajar. He slipped inside.

* * * * *

When Cob Joiner discovered a cat huddled beside the door, left ajar when his apprentice went to fetch water, he shouted at it and tried to shove it out again with his foot, but the cat, hurt though he was, dodged the foot and took refuge under a worktable, where the joiner could not reach him. The man shouted for his wife, who came, kitchen ladle in hand, and when she saw the cat she shouted back at her husband. "Dumb-pate! Can't you see the poor little beast be hurtin'? Leave be, man. Leave be and go eat your porridge."

"Hurtin' or no hurtin', it's out o' here for a cat with 'er nasty claws. Here, you varmint, out! Get out!"

He got down on his knees with some trouble, because he was growing old and getting stiff in his joints, and reached for the cat with his right hand. Toy, terrified, hissed and struck out with his right paw, claws unsheathed.

"God ha' mercy! 'Tis a wild beast. An' I be bleedin'." He held his hand up to his wife, who showed him no sympathy.

"Get up! Get up, man! Go wash yer hand and put a bit 'o onion on it. Yer porridge's in the bowl a-coolin'. I'll get t' little beast."

She helped her husband to his feet and out to the kitchen, where she ladled some of the porridge out of his cooling bowl and took it back to the workshop. The cat had moved from his position under the worktable and was cowering behind a half-finished coffer.

The woman sat down on a low stool. She was stout, and the tendrils of gray hair that she fingered back under her coif were damp with perspiration. She swayed a little from side to side as she began to speak softly, gently to the cat.

"Come, Pusskin. Come, Pusskin. See what I have here. Come, Pusskin, and see. Come, Pusskin, and see. Be not afeared, no, be not afeared. Come, Pusskin. Come Pusskin. Be not afeared."

She bent over and laid the half-filled ladle on the floor in the straw. And she continued her spoken chant, swaying ever so slightly from side to side.

Toy had not eaten for more than forty hours, but he was too hurt and too frightened to take the food. He heard the soothing voice and he relaxed a little, but he still feared to show himself.

The old woman was about to give up when Toy's need overcame his fear. He crawled out from behind the coffer. He eyed her and he eyed the ladle. Slowly, he came, belly to floor, a few paces at a time, looking from woman to ladle and back again. When he reached the ladle the old woman stopped swaying.

She sat stone-still but continued her low whispered chant. "Come, Pusskin, come, Pusskin. Don't be afeared. Come, Pusskin, come, Pusskin. Don't be afeared."

He sniffed the ladle, then his tongue explored the contents. It was warm and soft. He licked the ladle dry, eyeing the old woman between licks.

He had to wash with his hurt left paw because he could not support his weight on it to use the other. When he finished washing he cautiously crawled over to the old woman and rubbed his forehead on her instep.

He felt a large, firm hand under his belly, and he was lifted up and held close against the woman's bosom. It was big and soft like the cushion in Cecily's chair. He began to purr.

* * * * *

The joiner's wife tended the cat's hurts as best she could. She put a tight bandage around his broken left front foot, and for three days he lay in a corner of the settle on a flour sack, scarcely moving.

And she discovered that he was not Pusskin but Tomkin, which she named him. But when she called, "Tomkin! Come, Tomkin!" he did not respond—until the time when she, exasperated, called "Tomkin, *Boy*!" His ears perked and he turned his head. Then he got down from the settle and limped over to her.

Dinner here was not the festive meal it had been in the merchant's house, nor was Toy allowed the freedom of the table. Cob and his wife and his apprentice ate their meals in the kitchen, where they also slept, for it was warm there from the cooking fires, and the other larger room was used as workshop and showroom by the joiner.

The joiner's wife, whose name was Megge, saved

scraps from the table for Toy. This was meager fare indeed, but he soon discovered the small creatures that slipped timidly by night out of holes along the place where the wattle-and-daub walls joined the earthen floor. And in spite of his wounded leg he managed to catch one and to taste it, and afterward he found mousing to be both a sport and a means of supplementing his spare diet.

But Cob fumed at the cat's continued presence in the house. "He canna' stay here. I will no' have a cat a-scratching on my woods!"

Cob brandished a gimlet at his wife, while his apprentice tried to clean up the mess from a gluepot Toy had overturned as he jumped off the joiner's work-table and fled into the kitchen. "He has na' caught a dozen mice yet, an' he makes stink in the straw on the floor! An' look you at this chest! Claw marks all down the sides. Get rid o' him, I say! Get rid o' him!"

* * * * *

Megge carried Toy upstairs to the Flemish weavers who lived on the floor above the joiner. The man, Wilhelm, and Freda, his wife, sat at their looms weaving fine cloth which made them if not warmly accepted at least tolerated in a foreign land.

"Ve giff you velcome, Mistress Megge." Wilhelm rose courteously, and Freda stopped her work and smiled up at the joiner's wife. "What haff you there?"

"God's greeting to you both. And I have here a cat, a hurtin' cat, him that needs a spot o' shelter and a bit o' porridge now and then 'til he be fit to fend for himself." She sat down on the stool that Wilhelm fetched for her and held out the cat for them to see. "My man be mean and hateful and will not let the cat bide by him. I seek a place where the poor little beast will be safe for a while."

Wilhelm took the cat from her and stroked Toy's head. His forefinger traced the "M."

"A fine cat it is, Mistress Megge. A beautiful cat. He vill be a noble animal, excellent and to be honored. But he has claws." He set the cat on the floor.

But Toy had seen the loom. He had seen the threads stretched enticingly, inviting him to touch and feel and spread his toes. As though he would demonstrate the weaver's objection to him, Toy jumped up on the loom and began to knead with his right paw.

Freda screamed and jumped up, overturning her stool. Wilhelm laid a firm hand on the cat's neck and plucked his claws from the threads. He handed the cat back to Megge.

"Yah, he cannot stay here. I see that. A pity it is. A pity."

Megge shook her head sadly and rose to her feet. She tucked the cat under her arm. "You be a wicked boy! Bad boy, bad *boy*! Bad *boy*, you be." He turned his head and looked up at her. "I do believe he knows what I tell him," she said. "Alack, I hate to part with him,

60

that I do." She made her way to the stairs which ran down the back of the building.

Wilhelm patted her shoulder. "Ve vish you vell, Freda and I," he said. "May good fortune go vith you— and the cat." And Wilhelm returned to his loom as Megge went lumbering heavily down the stairs.

At the bottom she stopped to watch Cob and his apprentice as they carried in from the courtyard what seemed to be the last of several loads, which they stowed in a corner of the workroom. She followed them.

"Ah! The Helle-Carte again," she said, eyeing the trestles and canvas and hoops and thin pieces of lumber stacked in the corner. "Will ye never be done with makin' it right, what those clumsy actors break every time there be a frolic?"

"Frolic, woman? You call it frolic to show folk what it be like come Judgment Day? The Guild be servin' the Lord's cause better'n those monks and friars for all their holy garb."

Cob spat into the straw as he pulled the Jaws of Hell from the pile and carried them to the worktable. Those jaws were a problem. They had to open just right when worked by a guild member concealed behind the stage, so that they could gobble the sinful down into hell through a trapdoor to the ground under the stage. Cob's task was to make sure all the parts were in working order before being assembled out in the courtyard.

The Helle-Carte stage was a platform made of

wooden planks laid across the top of a wagon which pulled the theatre through the streets of Norwich on holy days and festivals. The wagon halted in market place or courtyard or wherever a crowd could assemble to watch. Members of the Joiner's Guild acted out a spirited show about the Last Judgment.

Megge laid the cat on his flour sack on the settle and gave him a piece of sausage skin which she had saved for him, then she sat down on a bench and watched Cob and the apprentice at work.

"Mind you the time," she reminisced, "when our young Diccon played a holy angel? And so he looked, all in his white robe with his yellow pate and a fine wire halo over his head? And, and,"—here she began to chuckle—"and he a-blowin' his trumpet so hard he tripped and fell straight into hell!"

She rocked with laughter and in spite of himself Cob began to chuckle also. He paused from filing one of the thin wooden teeth where the point had broken off.

"Aye! And I mind me how those lost souls in their striped tunics gave such trouble to Satan, a-pullin' on his hairy coat and red beard and his horns and tail till it looked they'd get the best o' him before the righteous ones could have a go at him with their brooms and staves!"

Toy jumped down from the settle and rubbed against Megge's ankle. Cob stopped laughing and scowled at him. "If I could bide that beast long enough, I'd put a chain on his neck and an ugly mask over his pretty face and then in the play one o' the actors could give his tail a sharp twist! And *there* we'd have a yowlin' demon to fright wicked folk back to their prayers!"

"You wouldna'! Cob, you wouldna' be so cruel to t' poor little beast!" Megge took Toy up onto her lap and stroked him.

"Aye, but I would! If I be not rid o' him soon, I'll carry him down to Wat Furrier. Mayhap we could use a catskin in t' show."

Megge did not believe her husband would really carry out his threat, but she knew that the cat must be disposed of in some way. She stroked him as she tried to think of what to do now.

Her lap was not like Cecily's lap. It was more like Cecily's bed or the velvet cushion in her chair. Cecily was not here. Toy had looked for her, but she was not here, nor was her soft bed or her chair with his beloved velvet cushion. Nothing here was like the home he had known since he was ten weeks old. Here there were no fresh rushes on the floor, only rough, prickly dry straw and sawdust. Here was no long table laden with food, no great cupboard with metal objects for him to knock around. Everything here was strange and hard—except the old woman. He wanted Cecily, but she was not here. She did not come to help him or to play with him or to cuddle him in her arms. He was afraid of Cob. He was afraid of the apprentice, 'though the apprentice had not kicked at him as the watchman or Cob had. He wanted Cecily, but Cecily was not here.

he light rain had ceased soon after midnight. Larks sang in the dawn, and pearly rose and misty gold gave way to streaks of yellow sunshine as the clouds broke up and blew in the wind like balls of lamb's fleece across the sky.

Megge held Toy in her arms as she stood, early in the morning in the midst of a crowd at the edge of a meadow, and watched a procession of oxen wearing flowery nosegays tied to their horns. They dragged the Maypole, garlanded with flowers and herbs and ribbons, to the center of the green. They were followed by young men and women and children singing and dancing, maidens shaking timbrels, boys and young men blowing huntsman's horns, children waving flowery boughs and branches of May blossoms.

The rain-washed air was like wine, and though the

May Day festivities were not yet at their height, the throng was intoxicated with the sheer joy of being outdoors in the bright, warming sun. The short, dark days of winter were over, thanks be to God and all his saints! Folk may now leave off their labors and revel for a day and a night—or two! And no sober-minded holy men could stop them, try as they would.

Megge was jostled by a chapman with a pack on his shoulder, who reached out a hand toward the cat.

"Ah, a lovey cat! You wouldn't be sellin' that beautiful cat in the market, now would you? Nay, surely you wouldn't be partin' with it, now would you? Ah, what a pity. So lovey a cat!" The chapman could tell by the way the old woman held the cat that she was fond of it.

"Nay, Goodman." She looked at the peddler closely. His lips were pursed and his eyebrows drawn up in sadness as he lightly touched the cat's head. "Nay," she said, "I look to find someone to care for him. See? He be lame. And I canna' keep him, for my man will not have a cat at home." She showed the bandaged paw to the man, who clucked and shook his head sorrowfully.

"Ah," he said. "The poor little one. He needs a gentle hand like my good wife's and a cushion by the fire and a well-filled bowl on the hearth. My good wife would love him to keep her company whilst I'm out about my business."

Megge looked down at Toy, then back to the chapman's long face. "And would you take him, then?

And see to his hurt? And keep him safe? He do mouse some, but he likes his porridge with a bit o' milk on it and a scrap o' meat or fish sometimes. Oh, I do hate to part with him, I do!" She cuddled Toy up against her face. She longed so to keep him. She held him up so she could look into his dark-rimmed, golden eyes and prayed a silent prayer that he would find comfort and safety and a loving home.

"As I would care for a baby, so will I care for this beautiful cat," the chapman said. He shifted his pack and held out his hands. "And my wife, she will be so happy—so happy."

As Megge handed the cat to the peddler, the man suddenly lifted his head and looked out over the throng.

"My wife," he said. "There she goes now, dancin' with that group of maidens. I must catch her before she be lost. Gentle creature that she is, she cannot find her way without me. I must—" And the peddler disappeared among the crowds of revelers.

Once fully out of Megge's sight, the man, who had neither wife nor hearth of his own, pulled a meal sack out of his pack, then grasped Toy firmly by the back of his neck. "Here be pig. And here be poke. And there be profit for me!" And he thrust Toy, squirming, into the sack.

* * * * *

Nick, with his two companions Kit and Robyn,

splendid in their best doublets with flowers stuck in their belts and sprigs of May in their caps, ran in and out among girls dressed in their prettiest kirtles with wreaths of flowers in their hair. The boys danced with those around the Maypole, pulling their hair, grabbing at their flying ribbons and laces, snatching kisses when they could and receiving slaps on their faces with exaggerated howls of injury. Shouts and excited laughter nearly drowned out the sound of bagpipes and flutes and hurdy-gurdies, and the minstrels hung their harps and gitterns on their backs and joined in the dancing.

The grass on the outer untrampled edges of the green, dry now in the warm May sun, offered a blossom-studded blanket to the boys who tumbled breathlessly down onto it with a young girl in their midst. She squealed and laughed as she struggled about with them, and when they relaxed their hold on her she did not run away but sat back on her heels and pelted them with fistfuls of grass and clover. She tossed her head and cuffed each boy in turn. She grabbed Nick by the hair. He caught her wrists and the two of them rolled screeching and laughing over the grass until the girl's mother bore down upon them.

"Ruffians! Villains!" the woman screamed. "By'r Lady, I should have you lads whipped! Be still, Alice, or I will have you whipped with them. Such disgraceful behavior! Mind you revel decently! Alice, come! Come away, I say!"

She pulled her daughter to her feet and dragged her, crying and protesting, away.

The other boys soon scrambled up and ran back into the crowd in search of further sport, but Nick sat on, there on the flowery grass, for the laughter had gone from him. The girl had pulled a blossom from the garland on her hair and struck his cheeks with it, pouting and blinking her big dark eyes. She looked the way Cecily might have looked if Cecily had lived some years longer.

Less than a week had passed since Nick had got leave from school to attend the child's funeral at the Church of St. Cuthbert. He had paid his condolences and respects to her father and had briefly greeted the apprentices and servants, but he then drew Nurse apart from the rest and they had walked together in the churchyard while she, between sobs, told Nick how the physicians had worked over the child, giving her all the finest remedies.

"Slime of gold mixed with slime of pearl, and ivory and saffron in holy water they gave her, but 'twas that foul cat sucked her life's breath out of her and their good remedies went for naught."

Nick had tried to reason with her and tell her that it was only an old, false belief that cats sucked children's breath, but she would not listen. To her, the cat was responsible for the child's dying, and she told Nick what she had done.

"For my poor Cecily's sake, God rest her little soul,

I forced myself to touch the devilish animal, and I flung him out into the street, and I hope he perished! I would never set eyes on him again—never! Nor on any of his loathly kind!"

Nick, horrified, had taken his leave quickly and wandered around the neighborhood, looking for the cat, calling, hoping to find a trace of him, searching in vain for a clue to his fate.

Even now, whenever he left the precincts of the Song School he found himself looking and calling, "Toy! Toy cat! Come, Toy!" It was hurtful for him to think of the kitten he had saved, the companion Cecily had loved, not being cherished and cared for anymore. He knew it would be a long time before he ceased searching for Toy.

As he sat on the grass of the May Day green, knowing that he should join again in the merrymaking, yet feeling now reluctant to do so, he remembered Cecily's answer when he asked her if Mother Julian had given her comfort. She had said, "Yes. I am not afraid anymore." He had wondered then at what she could have been afraid. Now, he was certain that she had been afraid of dying, like her mother, of the lingering, wasting Mediterranian disease. And Mother Julian had comforted her so that she was no longer afraid. Had Mother Julian told her that she would not die? Nick did not think so. He remembered something Mother Julian had told him, something that had helped him to be patient with his lot at the time: we are not promised that nothing will ever happen to us (he remembered her words "be discomforted") but that if trouble or disaster comes to us, we will not be overcome.

Cecily had been comforted.

Nick wondered if Mother Julian had learned of the child's death. He thought that she would want to know. She cared.

He would go now and tell her of it. And thank her again for all the help she had given to each of them.

As he jumped to his feet he was jostled by a peddler who seemed to be in a hurry.

"God ha' mercy, lad! You be sitting quiet as a stone and of a sudden you pop up like an arrow shot out o' the ground." He was carrying a sack that seemed to have something alive within by the movement and the sounds of it.

"I am truly sorry," Nick said. "I beg you to pardon me." Then he could not help asking, "What—what is it that you carry there?"

" 'Tis but a pig," said the man, "A suckling pig for to sell. Be it no concern of yours!" And he hurried away. But even as Nick looked after him, thinking that he had never heard a pig sound so much like a cat, the man stopped.

There was a tearing sound. The man swore and dropped the sack, and raised a bleeding hand to his mouth.

A yellow cat burst out of the sack and ran past Nick—swiftly, though it ran on three legs.

For a moment Nick just stared. Then he ran after the cat, calling, "Toy! Toy! Is it you, Toy?" But the cat disappeared into the crowd. Nick continued to call and to search, without finding. Perhaps it was not Toy anyway. Toy ran on four legs, unless—. Again Nick searched and called and searched and called, to no avail. Because of all the noise and confusion, he finally gave up and turned his steps towards Lady Julian's anchorhold.

* * * * *

Toy dashed among the crowds in mindless fear of the peddler and his sack.

He dodged in and out among the feet of dancers and onlookers. A boy caught him by the tail and tried to pick him up. He turned and bit the boy, who let go of him, and ran on. At the far edge of the green he ran toward a clump of trees. Instinctively, he tried to run up the trunk of one, but here his bandaged left foot impeded him and he fell back to the ground. An abandoned flower-bedecked wheelbarrow stood against a tree. He ran underneath it and cowered there, shivering in fear.

He stayed crouched under the wheelbarrow for a long time, but no people came near to disturb him and finally he began to relax. At nine o'clock the cathedral bell rang out the hour of Terce. Carts drew near and folk set up their counters and booths of foodstuffs. Whelk-sellers, bakers, vendors of hot meats and cooked fish began calling out their wares:

"Hot sheep's feet! Hot sheep's feet."

"Tasty ribs o' beef! Come buy, come buy!"

"Pork! Hot pies! Sausages for your dinner! Come buy!"

"Fine rolls o' bread!"

"Good ale from the Bull's Head Tavern! Come wet your throat! Come buy."

Hungry customers, pennies in hand, came crowding around: noisy, laughing young men and maidens, older folk with children, all garlanded with flowers of May, all a-burst with joy of sun and warmth and freedom from toil for a day.

No one noticed the abandoned wheelbarrow. Tense and disturbed as he was by the noise, the cat feared even more to expose himself to the sight of people, and he stayed where he was.

* * * * *

At three o'clock, when the cathedral bell rang out the hour of None, some folk, mostly older men and women, had thrown themselves on the ground and were snoring, while the younger ones were back at the Maypole or had slipped away, by couples, into the woods. When a man came reeling over to the wheelbarrow and vomited against it, Toy crawled out and

73

ran behind the nearest food stall. It belonged to the fishmonger, who sat on the ground on the far side of it in its shade, drinking his ale and patting the money pouches fastened to his belt. All that was left of his wares were the empty barrels behind the cart.

Soon he clapped the cover over the last open barrel, lifted them all up onto the cart and started home to his shop by the Wensum River. The barrel he covered last contained fish scraps. And a cat. Toy, not quite quick enough this time, was—unknown to the ale-drowsy man—trapped inside.

he best that could
be said of life for a cat along the riverfront was that there
was food a-plenty—if a cat could compete for it and hold
his own against the other cats who prowled about. After
a day or two, Toy had a ragged ear.

He sat on top of the fishmonger's stall and with his
teeth he pulled hard at the bandage the joiner's wife had
wound around his left paw. (This was a mistake, because
if he had left the bandage there it might have kept the
broken bones in his foot from mending crookedly and
leaving his paw misshapen for the rest of his life; but
the bandage was tight and worrisome to him and he
finally pulled it off.) Then he washed and washed the
lame foot and was still washing it when the fishmonger
saw him and yelled at him. He jumped down and ran
off. But he would be back. The fishmonger, like the

merchant's cook, yelled at him often but also threw some tidbits his way.

That was all there was in his life now that resembled his life before. There was no one now to pet him or cuddle him or play with him. There was no soft cushion for him to curl up on and knead with his paws. There was no shelter for him, except what he could find for himself when he needed refuge from rain or people or other animals. He had no home.

Most of the people he encountered yelled at him or tried to kick him or grab him, and he became wary of humankind. And he learned to hold his own with cat-kind. He learned to fight when he had to. Sometimes he roamed peaceably with other cats and he learned from them. He learned by smell which territory belonged to another cat, and he learned how to leave his mark on what seemed good to him, on what he wanted for his own. At night he learned how to get up on top of something and howl, and he learned how to dodge whatever was thrown at him.

He spent much time in the middle of King Street rooting with other animals for scraps of food in the garbage. When he walked (he didn't walk very much) he limped on his left front foot, but when he ran or leaped to some high place, his lameness was only barely noticeable. He did not know he was handicapped.

* * * * *

Nearly two months of straying and prowling had gone by when, one day, he found his way up the hill to the garden by St. Julian's Church. He jumped onto the wall and looked over.

Below him an old woman was on her hands and knees digging around a bed of pansies. He stretched out on top of the wall and watched her. She looked up and saw him.

"Ha, cat—a yellow cat!" she said. "Mind you don't come a-scratchin' up Lady Julian's flowers! She loves her flowers and she needs have some sweetness and color to look out on to refresh her for her prayers—if folk would only leave her any time for praying!" This last she added as the bell sounded at the gate.

He lay on the wall and watched as the old woman got to her feet and went to the gate.

"Ah, 'tis you, Nick Tanner. Mother Julian will speak with you whenever you come. But, I pray you, don't keep her long." She opened the gate but Nick did not come through.

"Thank you, Sara," he said. "I will not disturb her today. I came only to bring her some flowering plants for her garden—sweet pinks from the cathedral beds where there are too many, or so said Brother Giles. He works in the gardens and he saved these for me to bring here."

"Dame Julian will love them I'm sure," Sara said. "They mind me of a garden I tended as a child. Thank you. You're a good lad. Nick. A good lad." She took the plants from him and set them on the ground. Then she turned back to Nick.

"I was saddened to hear of the little maid's dying," she said. "I mind me the day you brought her here, poor little lass."

"Yes," Nick said. "She had much comfort from Mother Julian that day. I believe it lasted for her until— until the end."

"Then I'm glad for her," Sara said. "And thank you for Dame Julian's flowers. God go with you, lad—and bless your studies. *You'll* be precentor one day, folk hereabout are saying."

Nick laughed and shook his head. "I just want to make songs and sing them," he said and took his leave.

* * * * *

There was something about this place and the sound of those voices across the garden that stirred a response in Toy.

If Cecily somehow returned to him, he would have recognized her, known her and greeted her with joyful love. But he carried within him no images to remember, only sensory responses. Anything pleasing that happened to him stirred in him a feeling of the goodness that was Cecily; anything soft was her cushion.

After Sara went inside, he jumped down from the wall into the garden. He explored the beds of lettuce and parsley, carrots and beets, and lilies, gilly-flowers and roses. The smells were rich and sweet to him. This was good. It was like some goodness he had known before. It was *good*. He rolled in the pansy-bed.

Sara came running out again.

"No, no, naughty cat!" she cried, and clapped her hands at him.

He stopped rolling and crouched on his feet, eyeing her.

He did not run.

This woman was not afraid of him. She did not dislike him.

There was no need to vex her.

Slowly, then, he approached her. He threw himself on the ground before her, rolled over on his back, and squirmed first to one side, and then to the other.

The age-old reaction was natural to them both: she bent over and rubbed his chest; he closed his front paws over her hand; brought his hind feet up, and playfully beat them against her arm.

"Well, then, well then, it's a fine cat, he is, a fine cat. Well, then; a fine cat, yes, yes, a fine cat."

No one had spoken to him like this for a long time, nor had anyone stroked and petted him since the joiner's wife gave him to the chapman.

" 'Tis a pity you roll in the flowerbed. Lady Julian needs those flowers—little catfaces, they are." She straightened and clapped her hands again. "Be off with you now. Go home—go home. Off!"

But Toy liked it here. He followed her as she walked toward the door. She turned and clapped her hands again.

"Shoo! Shoo, cat. Shoo. Go on home. Go on home!"

He jumped onto the windowsill and rubbed against the side. Then he rubbed against the black curtain. It gave way and he was about to nose his way under it when Sara took hold of him and pulled him off.

"No! No! You must never disturb the Lady Julian! Bad boy! Bad *boy*!"

He turned his head and looked up at her.

"You understand? Do you? Now you mind what I say!" She crossed the little garden and set him on top of the wall. "Go home! Go back where you belong! Go! Go!" And she gave him a shove, gentle but strong enough to send him over the wall to the ground on the other side.

He would have jumped right back up and back into the garden again, but a field mouse ran along the bottom of the wall, and he chased it instead.

* * * * *

After Toy caught the field mouse and ate it, he strayed in a northerly direction until he came into Parmentergate, the street of the parchment-makers and leather-workers. There one of Wat Furrier's men saw him.

The man spoke to the cat and Toy looked up at him. He *did* like having his chest rubbed. He threw himself down and squirmed on his back.

The hand that came down on him did not rub, it grabbed. The cat's front paws, claws unsheathed, closed hard over it, and scratched; his hind feet struck hard, digging the claws deeply into a smelly arm.

The man swore, pulled back his hand, and kicked at the cat. Toy evaded the kick and dashed away.

He continued to move in a northerly direction until he found shelter under a hedge by the Church of St. John Evangelist. There he made himself comfortable and slept the rest of the day.

After curfew, when humankind were no longer about, he wandered around Gray Friars' Priory.

It was a great night for cats.

Every now and then the wind drove dark woolly clouds apart to reveal the sight and brilliance of a full moon.

Toy prowled about, sometimes with other cats, sometimes contending with other tomkins for a pusskin's favors, sometimes alone, leaving his mark on territory new and pleasing to him. Dawn and the bells of the Angelus found him in the porch of St. Cuthbert's church. At six o'clock when the bells rang for Prime he was stretched out on the top of the cathedral wall near St. Ethelbert's Gate, fast asleep.

PART III

OME

he ten boys in the Song School sat on stone seats in the east walk of the cloisters waiting for the precentor, Brother Wilfred, to come and hear them rehearse special music he had composed for the Eve of St. John the Baptist. Nick and Kit, instead of working on the *Kyrie*, were playing a game of noughts-and-crosses on one of the stone desks. The succentor had been drilling them all for days, but now he took Robyn aside and was working alone with him on a passage in the *Gloria* which Robyn was supposed to sing, his beautiful voice soaring above the rest. But today Robyn's voice did not soar. It cracked and the succentor was beside himself.

"Today you break! *Today*! Could you not wait until after St. John's Day to change?" The succentor beat his fist on the side of the small portable organ. "Holy Mother of God! After all my pains with you! Try again—and don't break! Now!"

"*Do-mi-ne Fi-li u-ne-ge-ni-te Je-su Chri-*" Robyn's voice broke again just as precentor Brother Wilfred joined them in the cloister walk.

"Ah, Robyn," he laughed. "That will never do!" And seeing the crestfallen look on the boy's face, he put his arm around Robyn's shoulders. "Don't let this cause you distress. You will be able to sing again—though likely not so beautifully. It happens to us all. Now you'd best concentrate on your Latin, and memorize as much liturgy as you can, and sing the offices as best you can. I need you, Robyn. I need boys to train to carry the music of the liturgy." He shook Robyn lightly. "A boy's education does not end when his voice breaks! And remember, you will soon be making your first vows to become a novice." He turned and looked around at all the boys.

"Nick! Kit! Which of you will be first to follow in Robyn's footsteps?"

The two jumped to attention. Kit grinned self-consciously and shook his head.

Nick stood frozen, mouth open, speechless. *Did Brother Wilfred expect him to become a monk, too?"*

The precentor chose another boy to lead the chanting on the morrow. When rehearsal was over and the boys were sent to do their chores, Nick rushed to find Brother Giles in the granary.

"Brother Giles! Brother Giles, I must speak with Mother Julian." Nick dropped down on the bench beside the old monk, who was mixing a bowl of mash and milk for weaning kittens. "Please, Brother Giles, please send me out on an errand that I may go to the anchorhold. Please!"

"But Nick." Brother Giles sat back on his bench and studied Nick's face. "You just visited the Lady Julian yesterday. Did she not help you then?"

"Nay, Brother, I did not speak with her at all. Sara said as I came to the gate—she must have been talking to herself, for I saw no one there—she said folk don't leave Mother Julian time for her prayers. And I saw no reason to disturb her, for I had nothing amiss—then— and no need of her counsel."

"And now, lad? Something troubles you? Something that I cannot help to ease?"

Nick looked away. He had not spoken with Mother Julian since the day he told her of the child's death. He knew that Brother Giles could give him loving advice. It was said of Brother Giles that he spent more time in prayer and meditation than any of the other monks, even that he was often wont to fall into a trance. Indeed, some of the novices were heard to say that they expected one day to see him levitate—rise clear off the floor in ecstasy. But Nick craved the special understanding, the words which always seemed to come from heaven itself, the soothing, healing voice of Mother Julian.

"It's just that—" Nick stammered. "That I am in need of—of *Mother* Julian."

"I think I understand, lad." Brother Giles smiled. He rose and picked up a shallow pan from the bench at his side and set it on the floor in the middle of the granary. Then he poured the contents of the bowl into it. It was immediately surrounded by kittens climbing over one another, pushing, nuzzling, stepping into the mash.

The old monk and the boy watched for a moment, then Brother Giles said, "Come, I have a small rosebush which I should have sent yesterday. Mind you are back by noon in time for Sext."

As they left the granary he sighed. "Complaints come to me from the master cellarer on down to the assistant spitboy if the cats get abroad." And he carefully closed the door.

* * * * *

As Nick ran through St. Ethelbert's Gate to get to King Street he did not look up. Had he done so he might have seen Toy up there on a ledge, washing himself.

* * * * *

"You would still make songs and sing them?" There seemed to be a smile in Mother Julian's voice. "But you are not happy in the Song School?"

"Oh, I *am* happy. I love the Song School. And I'm learning more of music than ever I dreamed of. Precentor

88

Brother Wilfred is having me study composition, and soon I will begin to learn to play the organ. I love it all—and being able to spend time helping Brother Giles in the garden, and in the granary, talking about cats—"

Nick stopped.

"What is it, Nick? What troubles you?"

"*I fear that Brother Wilfred expects me to become a monk!*"

"And that frights you?"

"Yes" Suddenly, Nick wondered how Mother Julian could understand, she who spent her life in what most people would consider a prison. How would she be able to understand how hard it was for him even to think of being held to such a strict rule all his life long?

"At the merchant's house at Christmas time," he began, "there came a minstrel, one who had traveled much and sung his songs in many houses, including the king's, where he heard a poet read about ordinary folk—a miller and a squire and a nun with her little dogs. I would compose and sing such songs, and travel about. And I would come back, and compose beautiful music, like that of Brother Wilfred's that we sing tomorrow for St. John's Eve. I think—" Here Nick turned and looked around from side to side and up and down again. He held his arms out wide. "I think I want it *all*!"

Mother Julian laughed.

It was warm, rich laughter, indulgent, not derisive. Nick felt it loosen the tightness within him. And he laughed with her, at himself and at the pleasure of hearing her.

"Ah, Nick," she said, laughter still echoing in her voice. "Be not woebegone and depressed. Nick, whatever you do, wherever you be, however you spend your days, live in this way, that is to say in longing and rejoicing. I was taught that love is our Lord's meaning. Some of us believe that He is almighty and *may* do everything, some that He is all wisdom and *can* do everything. But that He is all love and *wishes* to do everything, this we fail to understand, and it is this that hinders us, as I see it."

She paused, and then continued, her voice now low and gentle. "During our lifetime we have in us a marvelous mixture of well-being and woe, but our life is rooted in love. It is His will that we have most faithfulness and delight in love. *All our travail is because love is lacking on our side.*"

She paused again. Then, "Remember this, Nick," she said. "If so be you sing your songs at the altar of the cathedral or in the king's house or in a tavern, offer them with love. Look upon all things, wherever you be, with the eye of your understanding and know that all shall be well."

Nick pondered her words in silence. Then, "Brother Wilfred has been kind," he said. "I hate to think that I might disappoint him—as I fear I disappointed the merchant."

"Then go and speak with Brother Wilfred and tell him how you feel," Mother Julian told him. "Go, Nick, and mercy and grace go with you."

* * * * *

After Terce on the morning of St. John's Eve, Brother Wilfred and Nick strolled together over the thick green grass in the enclosed square of the cloister garth. For a few moments they watched workmen arranging slabs of stone in the northwest corner, finishing the rebuilding of the cloisters.

"It will be good, someday, to have the cloisters wholly renewed, and finally to be rid of that smell of burnt wood which has lingered here these many years." Brother Wilfred turned to face Nick. "And now, what is it that troubles you, son?"

Nick did not know how to begin—or what to say once he had started. He looked up into Brother Wilfred's kind face and blurted, "Must I become a monk? Brother Wilfred, *must* I?"

"Why, no, lad. Not if you do not wish to." He smiled. " 'Tis a good life—a good life for most of us. Why think you that you may not find it so?"

"I don't know. I'm sure it is a good life, only—I want just to make songs and sing them, and—and to be free and—" Nick looked down in confusion.

"You may make your songs and sing them," Brother Wilfred said. "It is my hope that you will learn to compose music for the holy offices and liturgies, as I do, surpassing me in the future. This you may do, whether you become a monk or no. That choice lies with you."

"Oh, Brother Wilfred, I should like that. I *should*. But I should also like to make songs about—well—about ordinary things like—like the watergate by the Wensum with barges going by; like the marketplace and common folk; like the peddlers and palmers; like those fellows working with stone in the cloister garth; like a dear old holy man like Brother Giles; and like a sad-eyed child— even a yellow cat."

"And about a merry little maiden named Alice?"

Nick stared red-faced and astonished at the precentor.

"Aye! I heard about Alice, from her mother. And much else besides about rowdy lads from the Song School." Brother Wilfred chuckled and shook his head. "I think that good dame would have liked to have us all flogged! Mind you," he added severely, "Never, *never* let your high spirits bring harm to anyone! Remember this when you are dismissed today after Sext: you may enjoy your St. John's Eve recreation for a few hours, but you boys will have an early curfew. I want you all back here for Vespers. You'll miss the bonfires, but 'tis as well. These revels become more boisterous and get more out of hand each year."

"Yes, Brother Wilfred."

"And remember, Nick. You may always train to

become a monk if you wish, but you shall never be compelled to do so. You have a long life ahead of you, by the grace of God, and many years, I pray, of good living in it. What may not appeal to you now may be the very same which will satisfy your needs in years hence. Now. Get you to the writing master. You must learn to letter well if you would write down those songs of yours."

In the scriptorium, where the monks copied manuscripts and, for several hours a week, taught the boys to letter, Nick came upon the writing master in a temper and the boys all laughing and whispering behind their hands in spite of the monk's efforts to bring them to order. Two of the boys were busy trying to wipe up a stream of red which ran down from the open shelves where materials for illuminating initial letters were kept.

"The master cellarer shall hear of this! Brother Giles must stand before the prior and answer for it this time!" The monk bustled about angrily gathering up some scattered squares of parchment from the floor. Nick noticed that some of them were marked with red spots. "These pages will all have to be scraped! Some of them may even need to be cut. Quiet, I say! Get you back to your lettering, all of you! Nick, why stand you there gaping? Get to your place and sharpen your quills! You all know this day's task: *Ihe - su mag - ne Rex ae-ter-ne. Jesus mighty King eternal.*"

He straightened for a moment and shook his finger

at the boys. "Remember: the "J" is now its own letter. No longer write "J" with two "I" 's, one on top of the other, except in Latin. In the English translation make the tail at the bottom curve gently to the left. If you cannot master this in one downward stroke, you may draw the curve with a fine-pointed pen. Look sharp to it. We've lost much time."

"What's amiss?" Nick asked Robyn in a whisper as he cut a quill and tested it against his forefinger. "Why all the mess? And what did Brother Giles do?"

"That holy old man? He didn't do anything. It was one of his cats. It stood watching us from the windowsill until the writing master saw it and sought to grab it. Then instead of jumping back out, it ran about in here sending the parchments flying and upsetting the jar of vermilion on the illuminator's shelf. He could not catch it and it ran out the door. You should have been here, Nick."

"What kind of cat?"

"A yellow cat." Robyn chuckled. "You should have seen it. You should have been here!"

hen the bell sounded for Sext, Toy was noising about under vestments hanging on a perch in the monks' dormitory. After a while he jumped onto one perch and from there to the sill of a small open window that looked out on the cloister garth. He could see nothing threatening there, only some figures in the far northwest corner, so he let himself down to a narrow ledge some three feet below. He was still much too high to risk a jump to the ground; and the ledge was narrow. He turned carefully and paced from one side to the other, but he was outside a cloister bay and jutting buttresses on each side hemmed him in. Just below him was an arch, and it projected about as far from the wall as the ledge he was on. Very carefully, testing the way on one foot after the other, he managed to get down into the spandrel, the space that formed a triangle in the corner over the arch. He crept down as far as he could and huddled in the lowest corner of the triangle just as the boys came rushing back into the east walk.

The boys tried to keep their voices down as they had been told, but they were in a hurry to get out and away to the St. John's Eve revels in Tombland. Toy, crouched in the arch outside, could not see them but he heard the muffled commotion underneath and stayed where he was.

When all was quiet again, he carefully slid down, front feet feeling the way, until he could jump the rest of the way to the ground. One of the workmen across the garth saw the movement, shouted, and started to walk over in his direction. Obeying his feline instinct to get under cover, Toy jumped back into the east walk. He crept along the shadow under the window seats.

After a while he sensed that he was not being pursued. He noticed some cupboards against the wall near a shallow flight of stairs. He could see books stacked inside and scrolls tied with strings, the ends of which dangled enticingly. Toy loved to play with things that dangled.

He jumped up into one of the aumbries and rooted around the books, knocking some of the scrolls out onto the stairs, where they bounced and rolled into the walk. He batted the loose strings with his paws, pulled on them with his teeth, swallowed the end of one until the scroll unrolled and fell to the ground, pulling the string back up out of his gullet.

The succentor emerged from the great church through the Prior's Door above the stairs, arms full of books and scrolls. Seeing Toy and the scattered scrolls, he shouted and tried to reach for the cat. He spilled what he carried, tripped, and sprawled face down among the scrolls.

Toy jumped over him, ran across the stairs, through the doorway, and into the cathedral.

Magnificent columns and soaring arches, delicate traceries, and exquisite stained glass, carvings and brasses offered no great pleasure to a little cat. But innumerable ledges, nooks, and niches did, and Toy made the most of them.

When the succentor came fuming into the south aisle, Toy watched him from the sloping sill of a narrow window above the monk's head. He watched until the man, angrily muttering, disappeared around the curve of the apse.

The cat indulged his love for high places, leaping, creeping, feeling his way for a safe jump, poking his nose into corners, rubbing his back around statues and inside niches, sniffing hangings prickly with threads of gold. He stopped for a short nap now and then, and a stretch and a wash, and then resumed his roaming.

It was a long while before he discovered the ancient Bishop's Throne. He sniffed and sneezed and nosed over the carvings in low relief around its base: the dove and dragons, the eagle and the tree, and the flames of hell were all to him only cold, rough stone. He stretched up on his hind feet and put his front paws on the seat.

Here was something else.

Here was a cushion!

He jumped onto the seat. He splayed his toes in ecstasy and began to knead. This was good! This was *good*! He put his face down into the cushion, purring deeply, kneading, kneading, gradually lowering his body, still kneading; even as he began to sleep, his toes kept spreading and kneading.

After a while he roused and stood up on the cushion. Arching his body high, he stretched his legs, front and back. He yawned, and then rubbed his side lovingly against the back of the throne, then turned and rubbed his other side. This was *good*! He raised his tail and left his mark upon it.

At that moment the succentor and the sacristan came in and saw him do it.

As the two monks rushed toward Toy with fists upraised, he jumped over the back of the throne and down into the east ambulatory.

He ran toward the south aisle, jumped onto a holy water font, found it too wet to hide in, and looked into the Chapel of St. John the Baptist.

Someone was there.

An old monk knelt there, very still, very quiet, not moving at all.

* * * * *

Brother Giles appeared to be in a trance.

The snow-white hair that circled his tonsure caught the light so that it looked like a halo in accord with the beatific glow in his eyes. He knelt gazing upward at the center panel of a painting at the back of the altar. In this center panel the Crucifixion was depicted, flanked by two panels on each side: The Scourging and the Bearing of the Cross at one side, and at the other, The Resurrection and The Ascension. All five panels were brilliant with color, vivid and graphic in detail, but Brother Giles's eyes were fixed upon the face of Christ on the Cross. And without sound or movement, Brother Giles was praying.

He was praying for the bishop who had given this painting to the cathedral. He was praying that the bishop might be forgiven for his worldliness and his militarism, for his persecutions and cruelties and severities. Brother Giles prayed that the monks would forgive him and the townsfolk would forgive him, and the peasants would forgive him, and that they all might be brought to remember that it was the bishop who had provided this beautiful painting for all men to see, and learn by, and meditate upon.

Brother Giles was not in a trance.

When he felt something soft rubbing against his legs, he unfolded his gnarled hands and, without a blink of his old eyes or a change in the tilt of his head, he sat back on his heels and stroked the cat. The cat pressed harder against him and began to purr.

Brother Giles was not in a trance, but many years of prayer and practice had provided him with the ability to appear to be in a trance so that troublesome monks might be more likely to leave him in peace.

When there was a noise in the south ambulatory, his hands became firm on the cat's back, and when sounds of muffled, barely suppressed anger and pursuing footsteps came nearer to the chapel, he slipped the cat under the skirt of his habit between his knees, folded his hands over it, and remained in this statue-still attitude.

"Brother Giles! Brother Giles, one of your granary cats is running loose in the cathedral. Have you seen it? A yellow devil-cat it is! A fiend—a little yellow fiend straight from hell!" The sacristan was breathless, puffing from anger and exertion. "He *sprayed—he sprayed on the Bishop's Throne!*"

"Aye!" The succentor wailed. "Aye, he did that. And he made havoc in the scriptorium and among the scrolls." The succentor poked about the small chapel. "Look you, behind the altar there," he said to the sacristan. "No? Well, he's somewhere hereabouts. I insist that he be caught."

"Come, Brother Giles. Come! You promised—remember? to keep those cats confined to the granary. Come, let us help you to your feet, Brother Giles?"

But Brother Giles appeared to be in a trance. He was praying fervently now that the cat would remain still and quiet.

"It's no use. You know Brother Giles and his trances!" The sacristan shook his head.

The cathedral bell began to sound the hour of None.

"What? Fifteen hours already? Nones *now*? Come, then. We will contend with Brother Giles afterward."

The two turned away and padded off in the direction of the choir.

"If Brother Giles misses holy offices *again*—"

"We have done all we can."

"We will have to tell all the brothers to look about for that animal."

"Brother Basil will drown it for us, once it's caught. I'm too tender-hearted to do that. But I do believe I could strangle it."

The voices became faint and fainter. Brother Giles waited until their sound died out and chanting had begun from the choir before he brought the cat out from under his habit and held him up like an offering toward the painting above him.

Then he tucked the cat under his elbow and managed with some difficulty to rise from his knees. As he shuffled quietly and as quickly as he could around the apse, behind the choir, along the south aisle and out the west door, he stroked the cat's head.

"You be no granary cat! And you be pure love despite your mischief," he whispered. "We must make haste, that I may be back before the brothers have done with None, else they may catch you. And they will punish you sorely. Our ancient Bishop's Throne is our greatest possession. It is good for you that you have nine lives— you do be in need of them all!"

Brother Giles carried the cat out into Tombland, noisy with cries of hawkers and peddlers, and lively with tumblers and mummers and minstrels among crowds of merrymakers all out to make the most of St. John's Eve: Midsummer's Eve.

Brother Giles stopped to ease his breathing. "If I set you free you will follow me back to the cloister. That is the way of cats. I know them well." He sat down on an empty wine keg outside a tavern and held the cat in his lap.

"Nick must be out here somewhere among the merrymakers. Precenter set the choristers free today from Sext to Vespers. If I can find him he will help to find a place for you."

Two youths burst from the tavern door, followed by a third whom the landlord thrust out by hair and collar.

"Get you hence, all of you!" shouted the angry host. "Troublemakers! Thieves! Knaves! Ruffians! Let me never see the like of you again!" He released his hold on the one, who reeled past Brother Giles and sprawled into the gutter. The landlord went back inside and slammed the door.

One of the knaves staggered over to Brother Giles. "What have you there, old holybones?" He leaned over unsteadily and grabbed the cat by the scruff of its neck from Brother Giles's lap.

"No! No! Don't do that. Give the cat to me, please." Brother Giles got shakily to his feet and reached for the cat. "Please, I beg you, I pray you, do not hurt it. Give it to me!"

But the knave held the cat squirming over the old man's head. "How come you by the cat, old holybones? It is *my* cat! My cat now! Aye—jump for it! Let me see you take it from me. Jump for it, holybones! Jump for it!"

Brother Giles reached for the cat, pleading with tears in eyes and voice. The young ruffian lowered it just within reach, then jerked it squirming and crying away.

The other knave now joined in the game. He grabbed Brother Giles by the shoulders and brought his red, sodden face close to the old man's. "Why, this be one o' cathedral monks!" he shouted. "Them as took a piece o' our forefather's marketplace for their shave-pates to play in. Monks ever be taking what's our'n, and we be poorer. That be truth and 'ee know it!" He spun the old man on his tottering feet one way. " 'Ee know it!" he said and spun him the other way. " 'Ee know—"

"Stop! Stop! Leave the holy one be!"

"Take your filthy hands off the old man! Shame. For shame!"

Two young men, students by their garb and tonsures, broke out of the crowd which surrounded the pipers and mummers and ran to the aid of the old monk.

The two knaves swayed shoulder to shoulder for a moment.

"Here come a pair o' know-alls!"

"We best be off!"

As the two ruffians ran off with the cat, Brother Giles fell and lay weeping on the cobbles near to the snoring knave in the gutter. The students gently picked him up and helped him along the way back to the cathedral.

ick and Kit and Robyn linked arms and sang a song not taught them in the Song School. They sang loudly, in a manner also not taught them in the Song School as they high-stepped away from a crowd around the mummers and joined the crowd around the jugglers. It was Robyn who noticed the two students break away and go to the aid of the old monk.

"Nick! Kit! Look you! That be Brother Giles!"

And the three ran and surrounded the old man and his rescuers.

"Brother Giles! You be hurt!"

"What's amiss? How came you here!"

"What happened? Tell us, please!"

"The cat!" Brother Giles managed to gasp. "Nick, go! Go get the cat! A yellow cat, a good little cat, so loving—" The old man burst into tears again. "I was trying to find you, Nick, to help find a refuge for the cat. That fellow wrested it away from me—they mean harm to it. I know they mean harm to the cat! Go find them. Try to save the cat."

Nick broke away and started off in pursuit of the ruffians. Kit followed him, and Robyn, after telling the students the way to take Brother Giles to the Infirmary in the southeast corner of the cloisters, raced to catch up with them.

* * * * *

The two knaves made their unsteady way through the Tombland throng. The fellow who carried Toy by the scruff of his neck said to the other, "Give me that latchet you took from the wench in the tavern. We'll tie this animal up with a stone and drop him in yonder well."

"Nay, it's good for a bit more sport. See here" and he pulled a tin spoon from his tunic. "I found more to steal than a paltry latchet. Methinks the cat be wearer o' both!" He tied one end of the latchet around the spoon, then the other around Toy's tail. "Now watch. This be better'n baiting a bear!"

Just as he pulled Toy from the other's grasp and dropped him onto the cobbles, the three boys caught up with them. Kit flew at one, knocking him to the ground and pummeling him furiously. Robyn went for the other, who tried to run but fell on his face when Robyn took a running jump to his back. Nick went for the cat.

Toy, crazed with fear, flung himself about in circles, rolling on his back in a frenzy to free himself from the spoon banging on the cobbles.

Nick got his foot on the latchet, and heedless of the clawings and scratches he got in the attempt, finally managed to grasp Toy firmly by the scruff of his neck. "Toy! Is it you, Toy? Is it you?"

But Toy was too frightened to heed, and continued to squirm and cry.

"Is that the cat you've been looking for?" Kit asked as he stood up, dusting off his hands.

"I think so. I think, I hope it is. But he's too frightened now. Kit, can you get that tin spoon off the end of the latchet? Good. Thank you."

Robyn joined them. "Is that your Toy, Nick?" he asked. "What are you going to do with him?"

Nick almost relaxed his hold on the cat.

What indeed *would* he do with him?

"I—I don't know. I think I must first get him calmed and quiet. I think I'll seek some quiet corner just to sit and—and try to soothe him. Robyn, you and Kit best go and look to Brother Giles. I will join you later."

Kit and Robyn turned back toward the cloisters. Nick, keeping a firm grasp with his right hand on the scruff of Toy's neck, managed to tuck the cat's body under his right elbow. Carefully, he put his left arm under the cat's chin, above the front legs, and grasped the hind feet in his left hand. Then he walked slowly out of crowded Tombland into crowded King Street. And as he walked he said, "Toy. Toy cat. Toy, Toy cat" over and over.

He turned away from the rowdy main thoroughfare onto a quiet lane, and when he came to a patch of greensward, he sat down, cross-legged with his back against a wall. He sat there, speaking softly to the cat, and after a time he began to relax his hold on the cat's neck. With that hand he gently stroked Toy's head. And as he stroked he began to sing very slowly, very quietly, the song he had made about Toy.

> "Fair dear cat of golden hue
> Softly "purr", softly "mew . . ."

When he finished the song he whispered, "Toy, Toy cat" over and over.

And after a while Toy turned his head and looked up at Nick.

Nick bent over and rubbed his cheek on the top of Toy's head.

"And now, Toy," Nick said, "what *am* I to do with you?"

All the weeks Nick had been searching for Toy, he had not thought of that. He could not keep him in the Song School. Toy could never stay shut up in the granary. Who could help him with a problem like this?

He stroked and cuddled Toy for a little while longer. Then he held the cat comfortably in his arms and walked back to King Street. Dodging in and out among the merrymakers, he turned his steps in the direction of the anchorhold.

* * * * *

Nick set Toy on the windowsill by the black curtain.

"Mother Julian," he said. "I pray you, forgive me, but I have here a cat, a very special cat, one I will always care for. I don't know what to do. Forgive me. I should not bother you with this matter. I should not have brought him here. But I don't know where to take him."

"Tell me about him," Mother Julian said. Her hand came out from under the curtain and stroked the cat. "He may be a cat of destiny." She laughed gently. "Tell me all about him, Nick."

"He has been sorely used—"

"And what is this attached to his tail?"

"A latchet. A cruel fellow tied a tin spoon to his tail. Here, I will remove the cord."

Mother Julian's other hand came up and held Toy by the neck, and she scratched under his chin while Nick untied the cord. Toy's tail switched it off the sill and down into the room.

"Poor little one!" she said. "He be in need of comfort, too. Tell me his story, Nick. I would learn about him, and, in the telling, more about you. Start at the beginning."

109

So Nick recalled that day of early autumn nearly a year ago and told her of his reluctance to drown the kittens and of his ruse in saving the yellow one and of the kitten's antics in the merchant's house. When he told her about the kitten's playing the Sacrificial Ram with the mummers she laughed richly, and he laughed with her in remembrance.

Meanwhile, as they talked, they relaxed their hold on Toy. He sniffed the black curtain. It seemed familiar to him. He pushed at it with his forehead and jumped down into the cell.

"Never mind," Mother Julian said. "He may explore freely. There is naught here that he can harm. And now, Nick, I would hear more about the cat."

While Nick talked, Toy sniffed around the cell. There was not very much for him to explore: a bed, a fireplace, a small table almost covered with books, a three-legged stool, and a little altar with a crucifix on it. A pilch, for warm covering in cold weather, hung on a perch near another window. He jumped up to the sill but the shutter was closed so he could not see Sara in the small adjoining room cutting up vegetables into pottage for the evening meal. There was one other window, a tiny squint looking into the church, but it had no sill big enough for him to jump onto. He jumped onto the bed and began to wash.

Nick told Mother Julian about the day he carried Cecily into the garden and sang the song about Toy, the day the precentor, Brother Wilfred, came and said that Nick might enter the Song School. And he told her about St. George's Day, the last time he had seen the child or Toy.

"And after the funeral, when Nurse told me what she had done to Toy, I searched for him, and I have been searching for him since that day, wondering if he survived. And now I've found him. It is he. He answers to his name—Toy."

"Let me see." Mother Julian turned from the window again. Toy was on her bed still washing.

"Toy," she called softly. "Toy, will you come to me? Come, Toy."

Toy stopped washing, got down from the bed, and came to her and rubbed around her ankles. She bent down and stroked him, then turned again to the window.

"And you cannot keep a cat in the Song School," she said. "Now that you have found him you must give him up. And you came to me—"

"Oh, Mother Julian," Nick interrupted. "I know this is not a matter to disturb you with. Forgive me. I just—I didn't know where to—I just seem always to come to you when I need help. Please forgive me!"

"Ah, Nick, there is not need of forgiveness. You have brought me joy in the matter! A matter of mercy and pity is of great concern to me. Mercy is a work of love, is it not? You and I know that the eye of pity is never turned away from us, and that mercy does not cease."

"Even for a little cat?" Nick was emboldened to ask.

"Love's concern is not only with things which are noble and great, but also with those which are little and small. Every kind of thing shall be well. The smallest thing will not be forgotten. You wish to find a home for the little cat?"

"Oh, Mother Julian, I can't give him to just anyone. I must find someone with love for him."

"Do not worry more. Toy seems to have found his own true home: He has taken up his abode with me. He lies even now curled up asleep on my bed."

Nick stood speechless in his sudden realization that Toy would be saved at last. Toy would have a home here, with Mother Julian! After all his efforts and concern for this cat's life it would be safe at last—with *Mother Julian*.

"Would you, then?" Nick said when he finally found his voice. "Mother Julian, would you let him live in your cell with you? I will help. I will bring you food. I used to share my milk with Toy's mother in the merchant's cellar."

"There is no need," Mother Julian laughed. "I have plenty to share with a dearworthy cat. The good people of Norwich bring gifts, and Sara sees to it that I am well served. But he must mouse as well!"

"He will. He will if it be only for sport. Of that I'm sure. But he will no longer need to fight—see his ragged ear?—or fend off dogs and pigs scrabbling for food in the middle of the street. But may he still be free to come and go? He is accustomed now to running free. He needs to be free. As I do."

"Yes, Nick. He may come and go freely through this window. May no more ill befall him."

"Surely no one would harm Mother Julian's cat!" Nick said. "Not if they knew—but how will folk know he is Mother Julian's cat?"

Mother Julian picked up the latchet and laid it on the windowsill. "I will loose the cords in this latchet. See? They are three, braided together. All is in three, Nick. All our lives are in three. All is in three." She made a circle of part of the latchet. "I will make a collar to fit him. The braid will expand as I slip it over his head."

"And all who see the collar will know that he is Mother Julian's cat? And can you tie a tag onto it, a little tag lettered with your name and his?"

"Alas, Nick," Mother Julian sighed. "Alas, I can not letter. The nuns did not teach us to letter when I went to school."

"I can letter! We're learning to letter in Song School. Allow me." Nick was overjoyed that there was another service he might do for Toy—and Mother Julian. "Please allow me to make the tag. I have the means at school, and I think I have the skill to do it. And Brother Wilfred has granted us free time tomorrow for St. John's Day as he did today for the Eve. I will come then, if I may, and bring the tag."

Nick ran all the way back to the cathedral, where Vespers had begun. The choir was well into the Psalm *Confitabor tibi* when he slipped quietly into his place.

other Julian sat on the three-legged stool in her cell and fingered the latchet. She loosened the braided cord, and at one end the three strings dangled from her hands.

Toy stood on his hind feet and batted at the strings.

"Patience, little one. This cord of your torment is now, for a moment, your plaything. It will become your safeguard, so that you may run freely without harm. Your little life must be glad and merry and sweet, lived in the fullness of joy."

She gently pulled the latchet away from the cat and measured a circle of it around his neck.

"If you are occupied with your dinner then I can finish your collar." She rose and poured a little milk into a wooden bowl containing the remains of frumenty from her meal, and set in on the floor.

"We shall make a pact, you and I: You keep my cell free of mice and vermin and I will share my food with you. And you may hunt outside. But mind you leave the birds be!"

After cutting the latchet, she sat down on the stool again and tied the ends of the small circle firmly together. And as she worked she continued to speak softly.

"All our life consists of three: our being, our increasing, our fulfillment. The first is nature, the second is mercy, the third is grace."

He did not understand her words but he understood the timbre of her voice—and the contents of the wooden bowl. He licked it clean. And after he washed he jumped onto her lap.

She stretched the braided collar over his head, then stroked him as he curled up into a ball.

" 'Tis well the *Ancren Riwle* comes down to an anchoress thus: 'Ye shall not possess any beast except only a cat.' There is love between us, little one. To this anchorhold you do bring joy."

He perked his ears and raised his head and looked at her.

* * * * *

The sounds of revelry from the street outside Mother Julian's anchorhold penetrated her curtain, and the noise lasted until long after curfew. The summer solstice gave added hours of light to the riotous festival of Midsummer

116

Eve. Merrymakers were loath to quit their carousal and return to the stuffy darkness of their homes for the night, even though the festival of St. John would last through the next day and the day after.

When Mother Julian knelt before her little altar and said aloud the psalms and prayers for the Vigil of St. John, Toy pressed against the soles of her feet.

When Mother Julian ate her evening meal, she asked Sara to bring her a shallow wooden mazer, which she filled with bread and milk and pottage and set it on the floor for Toy.

When Mother Julian lighted a candle and read from one of the books piled on her table, Toy curled up in her lap.

When Mother Julian blew the candle out and lay down on her bed to sleep, Toy got onto the bed with her.

She set him on the floor on a meal sack she had folded for his bed, but he got back onto her bed. She set him on the floor again, and again, and again, and again.

Finally, as the last sounds of revelry outside died away, she drifted into sorely needed slumber. Toy burrowed under her elbow, put his head on her shoulder and his paw on her neck.

* * * * *

The next day Nick returned, bringing with him a small vellum rectangle carefully lettered on one side thus:

J
U
L
I
C A T
N
S

On the other side was lettered the cat's name.

But as Nick passed the tag under the curtain to Mother Julian, he looked again at the cat's name as he had lettered it and cried out in dismay.

"Oh, Mother Julian, I have made a mistake. Look at the back. Forgive me, Mother Julian!" he cried. "I will make another tag. In my haste—we have been studying the letter 'J'—in my haste, instead of curving the tail at the bottom of the 'T' to the right, I drew the curve to the left. I will make you a new tag tomorrow."

"Yes, I see," came Mother Julian's voice through the curtain. "You have lettered a 'J' instead of a 'T'," she said slowly.

"I am so sorry! I only noticed the mistake now as I passed the tag to you."

Mother Julian's rich laugh rang through the curtain.

"Be not sorry, Nick! Oh, be not sorry at all—for you have lettered the name rightly. Your hand was guided as you wrote that name! This small creature began his life as "Toy," but that is no proper name for a cat of destiny! For the joy he brought to a dying child, and for the joy he will bring to me, henceforth that shall be his name: Joy."

Joy perked his ears and jumped onto the windowsill of the anchorhold.

J
O
Y

He liked the anchorhold. He liked the garden. He liked Sara. He liked to prowl for a few hours at night and come home through the curtained window at dawn. He liked to spend the day pressed against Mother Julian's feet as she knelt at her prayers; on her lap as she read; by her shoulder as she slept. When she stood at her window speaking through the curtain, he rubbed around her ankles. He loved her. She was his person.

He did not understand why she objected when he left his mark around the cell.

After a few days, Sara went in search of Nick.

"Lad," she said. "There be something to be done. I mind me when I was a girl, when the barber fixed our cat. Can you see to it, for the love of Mother Julian?" And she told him of the problem within the cell.

And Nick knew well what she meant. It had been Nick who, in penance for overstaying the Midsummer

Eve curfew, cleansed the Bishop's Throne with alkali and vinegar. "For the love of Mother Julian, that I will," he said. He would bring the cat to Brother Giles. Brother Giles understood well the ways of cats.

So it was that Joy lay on a bench in the cathedral granary between Nick and Brother Giles. There had been a moment of shock and unpleasantness and pain. Then Brother Giles comforted him with much caressing and a morsel of fresh raw oxliver, which Nick had been sent to fetch from the kitchens.

"And now, alas! He will father no offspring in his likeness. But to be Julian's cat must be his endless bliss!" Brother Giles supressed a laugh. "And the Bishop's Throne may be safe from him now, for he will likely bide happily in the anchorhold and not stray far from Mother Julian."

Back on Mother Julian's lap in the anchorhold, Joy purred in possessive contentment, lulled and comforted by her voice.

He did not understand her words, but he understood and loved the sound of her speaking, whether she spoke directly to him or through the curtain to someone outside.

*　*　*　*　*

As the years went by, Joy roamed Norwich less and less and stayed more and more within the anchorhold. In their life together he gave Mother Julian trouble only once. That was when a lady named Margery Kempe came to visit. She stayed too long. Joy marked what he felt to be Mother Julian's neglect of him by leaving the cell and sulking hidden under shrubbery in the garden, and Mother Julian missed him sorely. When after two days and two nights a cold rain began to fall, he relented and returned to the cell.

He lay by Mother Julian's feet when she knelt in prayer. He sat by her feet when she spoke through the curtain.

At times she spoke to him as she stroked him gently, but most of their communication was silent. In the peculiar rapport between cats and their persons, words have never been of great importance. But in Mother Julian's counsels of love were words of meaning for Joy had he been able to understand them.

"All natures in different creatures are all in man. We are always preciously protected in one love. Everything is penetrated, in length and in breadth, in height and in depth, without end:
And it is all one love."

All one love.

One love.

Love.

He understood.